Germaroon

Novel by
BILL FAIRBAIRN
GEORGE ATANGA

GERMAROON

ISBN 978-1-927481-62-2

BILL FAIRBAIRN
GEORGE ATANGA
2013

Also by Bill Fairbairn:

ON THE RUN IN AFRICA
THE PRINTER'S DEVIL

Printed by Documents Majemta Inc.

Published by:
Baico Publishing Inc.
E-mail: info@baico.ca
Web site: www.baico.ca

Cultural differences

The exploration of cultural differences in this novel represents a past and predicts a future that is relevant to all who live in this comparatively small planet. It tries to tell us that W.H. Auden's words ring true today

'All I have is a voice
To undo the folded lie
The romantic lie in the brain
Of the sensual man in the street
And the lie of authority
Whose buildings grope the sky
There is no such thing as the state
And no one exists alone;
Hunger allows no choice
To the citizens and the police
We must love one another or die'

Prologue

The atmosphere around Ntafoang Church in Cameroon heralded a big wedding. The bride and groom's family members wore gorgeous long dresses and smart suits with flowers in their lapels. Children in pretty dresses or shorts ran hither and thither. Three choral groups rehearsed near the church entrance. With lively melody and song they intended to accompany the bride up the aisle to the waiting bridegroom.

It seemed the happiest day of his life lay ahead of Daiga. He had returned home rich and university educated to Cameroon from the Federal Republic of Germany to marry his childhood sweetheart Mungwi. With a degree in political science from the University of Stuttgart he was poised for a diplomatic job in the Cameroon Ministry of Foreign Affairs. Daiga looked as elegant as any young man of 30 years could look. Everything from his white suit, the red carnation in his buttonhole and his shiny black shoes fitted well. No one could have mistaken the bridegroom among the scores of suit wearers mingling and talking or, behind Daiga, seated in the front row of the church awaiting the late arrival of the bride.

Mungwi had waited patiently four long years for her fiancé to return home. She had almost lost hope of ever seeing him again when told by one of his student friends he had married the daughter of a German business magnate and intended to stay in Germany. Even then she had kept him right or wrong tucked away in her broken heart not bearing to look for any man who could fit the qualities Daiga had left solidly in her mind. She had held up bravely rejecting a bevy of suitors until his letter told her he was coming home and asking her to arrange their wedding. She had joyfully awaited his return irrespective of stories told her of his infidelity in Germany. Her wedding day was for her a dream finally come true.

A wedding day tradition was that the bride should tactically delay her arrival at church to give concern to her waiting groom. Mungwi's arrival was a little too much delayed. The choir groups, the pastor and the bridesmaids were already growing bored with waiting and even tired under the hot sun. The earlier excitement was giving way to curiosity and nervousness about this act of marriage

The groom shivered as he fumbled with his handkerchief to wipe from his brow intruding drops of sweat. He could understand that Mungwi was keeping him waiting but why so long. He visualized everyone's eyes turned in one direction hoping to see the Mercedes Benz he had hired to carry Mungwi and her family. The delay was deliberate. It was having the desired effect on Daiga. Had Mungwi not waited four years for him? She had a friend in church monitoring Daiga's reaction. She would find out later the degree of his worry and later tease him about it.

Suddenly things happened so fast that no one knew what was going on. The bell in the church tower began to chime rapidly the moment the Mercedes Benz carrying Mungwi appeared from Prescraft Street and headed for the churchyard. Inside the church something peculiar suddenly happened. As the bell chimed a roughly dressed and dirty looking boy rushed up the aisle and from behind whispered something in Daiga's ear. Diaga turned abruptly and to his cousin Willy, standing proudly by his side and his best man, Daiga, in turn whispered: "I must go. I must attend to something now. I'll be back in a minute."

"No!" protested Willy. "Your bride has arrived. See the Mercedes drive in. You can't leave now with Mungwi almost at the church door."

"Don't worry," insisted the groom. "All is well." And off he went with the urchin to disappear behind the church building. The church bell stopped chiming. The choirs took over with "Here comes the bride" and proceeded with the minister into the church. The bride, accompanied by her father and mother, maid of honour and bridesmaids, entered behind them then were led the way to the altar. Mungwi raised her downward cast eyes looking for Daiga then stared at the empty seat reserved for him should he need it. Her heart sank when she realized he was not there to receive her. She quickly ran her eyes along all the seats of the front bench but Daiga was nowhere to be seen. She presently took a seat waiting with trepidation knowing Daiga was always up to something. Soon the congregation was quiet and the choirs seated. The presiding pastor raised his hands questioningly. Willy did much the same thing then ran up the aisle and out of the church in a panic before turning in the direction he thought Daiga and the urchin might have taken. The congregation waited in a silent trance as minutes ticked by. What was becoming clear to everyone present was that Daiga was not where he should have been. After almost

15 minutes Willy ran back panting to be met with an avalanche of questions.

"Where is he? Have you not seen him? The bride is waiting. Is the groom coming?"

"Is he not back?" responded Willy in a deep voice that reached the ears of everyone in the church. "Is he still not here? Then I don't know where he is."

There was fidgeting in the church as words passed from mouth to ear along the pews that the groom was missing. Two men from the congregation accompanied the best man out for a second search. After a short time five others followed the two. By this time the congregation was in disarray. The bride tried to rush out too, her father, trying to console her from tears but not knowing what to do or say. He finally urged her to wait.

"Where is Daiga? What has happened to him? What game is he up to?" she asked in consternation cradled in her father's arms at the church door and to his dismay muttering over and over: "I should never have agreed to marry him."

Questions were on the lips of everyone in the church. Little did they know that Mungwi's wedding crisis was the result of a wicked avenging scheme hatched 6,000 kilometres from Ntofoang Church in the Germanic land of the Caucasian race.

Chapter 1

PARIS HERE WE COME!

The bell rang out and a uniformed attendant announced: "Ladies and gentlemen, we are beginning our descent on Paris. The time is 6.20 p.m. and the airport temperature seven degrees centigrade. Tighten your seat belts and extinguish any cigarettes. Touch down is due in about five minutes. In a short time it will be supper time for you in the City of Light."

Daiga's heart leapt in anticipation and he adjusted himself in his seat to tighten his seat belt. Only he and God alone knew what clandestine plans he had for Europe. One of his classmates, Louis Jaguar, sitting next to him, tapped him on his lap and said: "Soon your dream will come true. You will be touching the white man's soil with your own two feet. What do you make of that?"

"Also the white woman with my own two hands and you know what," Daiga boasted. "I can't wait to get hold of first a French then a German woman."

"Lecherous beings like you can't think of anything better than another woman in your life," another classmate, Maria, scolded him from behind. "Remember you have left your fiancée back home in Cameroon. She will expect you to stay true to her. Mungwi will probably be thinking of you right now."

"Mungwi is far away in Africa and we are in Europe. Now it is the turn of the white Mungwi."

All but Maria laughed at his callous joke as the aircraft deadened its noisy engines and made a sharp turn on its downward glide to Orly Airport. Through the small window Daiga could see multi-coloured lights from skyscrapers and streetlights on expressway roads and he took in a dim glimpse of the River Seine.

"Europe is 100 years ahead of Africa. Compare this with what we have back home," he commented.

"The white man surpasses us in almost every way," agreed Paris, also sitting behind Daiga. "The white man has left us in his tracks and he makes the most of it."

"Be sure to drop a card to Mungwi the moment you leave the aircraft," instructed Maria seriously. "She is expecting you to write. She will be lonely already. I'm not so sure Europe surpasses us. Let us wait and see proof of that down below."

"You should remember to drop to Nameh."

"Of course."

The wheels of the aircraft bounced twice before screeching on the tarmac. After taxiing to Exit 27, it halted. They dragged out their bags from overhead bins and prepared for customs, immigration and health checks.

There were altogether nine students from the Ecole Normale Superieure of Bambili flying to different European countries for nine-month language courses. Six of them were to remain in France while two would continue to Spain. Daiga, who had chosen to study German, was bound for Stuttgart,

West Germany. All of them were due to spend two nights in Paris before continuing to their different destinations.

Administrative control took an unnecessarily long time in Daiga's opinion when he reached the immigration desk. Finally he was curtly told his visa was for West Germany, not France. The French immigration officials seemed reluctant to permit him to enter France. The six who had valid French visas passed through without trouble. Two bound for Madrid were detained together with Daiga for similar reasons.

"We can't let you into France, sir, you do not have the correct visa," the immigration officer coldly informed Daigo.

"I do not intend to make a home in France. I just wish to buzz around with my friends for a day to learn about Paris before continuing to my destination in Germany."

"Not possible. You must continue your journey to West Germany immediately and use your German visa there."

"I am on my way to Stuttgart to study German and have no wish to stay longer than two nights in France. You have my word for it. I can't afford to stay here for any length of time. Nine months of studies await me in Stuttgart. My airline ticket tells you my final destination is Germany and that is where I intend to go the day after tomorrow."

"We can't permit entry to France without a valid French temporary tourist visa. Most of your friends have the legal documents and by now have legally entered France. If we let you enter without a proper visa we may never trace you again. You must go direct to West Germany from this airport or, if you wish, return to Cameroon."

Daiga was immensely put out at the turn of events. He had hoped to spend two nights in a French hotel and describe his impressions of France on postcards to Africa. He mused over how things had started going wrong right from the start of the flight. They were supposed to have stopped over in Geneva, but the route had been changed before their departure. He had wanted his journey to be easy and educational all the way to Stuttgart. The immigration officer, who had spoken good English, dismissed more protests and turned to instruct two other officers to escort the three Africans back to the transit hall. Daiga's friends taking French studies had left without a word. He felt like crying at their abrupt separation and loss of his adventure in Paris. Now he was separated from his two other comrades as they were conducted separate ways.

One of the two summoned officers was black and Daiga sensed his French accent was different from that of his colleagues. He had been aware since his arrival that the fast French spoken by those he had met was filled with gap-fillers, omissions and contractions. He had difficulty understanding even this fellow black who was struggling to converse with him in French. He was constantly asking pardon and his negatives were never completed omitting the ne to je sais pas, j'ai pas de. Daiga finally asked him if he spoke English.

"Why no temporary tourist visa?" the man finally asked in English to Daiga's relief.

"I did not think of one for France. My stay here was to be informal and brief."

"Pardon me asking," the officer remarked while conducting him to the Air France desk to book an onward flight to Germany. "But who would pay for your stay in Paris if you were allowed a stopover?"

"The Cultural Attaché of the Cameroon Embassy of course. I mean the embassy itself."

"You mean it?" the uniformed man halted in surprise.

"We are students here on Cameroon government sponsored scholarship language courses in Europe."

"Do you mean that your embassy knows you are passing through France and expects you to stay over for a short time?"

"Yes, that is how I understand it," said Daiga, shrewdly adding that someone from the embassy likely might be waiting nearby to take them to a hotel. He won't be amused by this carry on. I expect he will formally object to your boss."

"Ooh, la la!" the officer broke out with a wide grin. "You are a lively one. Maybe I can help you if you keep quiet for a moment." He spoke to his white colleague in French then turned to Daiga. "Did the checking officer know about this?"

"He was very busy and more interested in the missing visas than in anything I had to say about why we were in Paris and who was sponsoring us. It seemed to me he wanted rid of us at any cost and get home to his wife for dinner."

On collecting their passports the black officer left Daiga and the two others with the white officer. After 10 minutes he returned and asked: "Which part of Cameroon do you come from?"

"Pardon."

"Which is your home town in Cameroon?"

"Bamenda. My two mates are from Mamfe."

"I was once in Cameroon, but I visited only Yaoundé and Douala," the man said. "Which is the capital city of Cameroon?"

"Yaoundé is the capital but Douala the bigger city," Daiga replied instantly knowing the officer was personally interrogating him in a rather juvenile way. "Why are you asking me those stupid questions?"

"I'll tell you what I can do," said the officer. "I'll put out a quick call on the loudspeaker for the Cameroon Embassy representative, if he is here, to go to the immigration checkpoint."

Daiga was marched back to the checkpoint and reunited with his two comrades and within a few minutes a distinguished looking black man came looking for them. Daiga guessed correctly that he was from the embassy and that he must have been waiting for all of them.

"Welcome to France," the man saluted them. "The rest of the party is nearby. I wondered what had happened to you. The loudspeaker told me you were having difficulties." Daiga glanced through the door left open by the diplomat and glimpsed his mates standing outside waving to him.

"We are very glad to see you. Can you tell this official we are here for study and just passing through France without intending to stay here?"

"What really is the problem?" the diplomat asked the immigration officer explaining that the students were of a study group arranged by Cameroon and French authorities to stay overnight.

"If your students were making overnight transit here in France why did they not have transit visas for France and Spain?" the immigration officer demanded to know.

"I take responsibility for my lack of a visa." Daiga cut in. "I told you that I did not think of doing that since I do not intend to spend much time here. Frankly, I did not know exactly what a visa was. There has been a mix-up."

The officer first glared at him but finally relented and gave each of them a card to fill in.

"What do we fill in as address of host in Paris?" Daiga asked.

"Fill in my name and address," the diplomat whispered, passing them his business card. They copied his name and address and, after passing the completed cards back to the immigration officer the man nodded. Soon they were on their way with airport red tape behind them. On joining their mates in the hall, Nambu joked extravagantly to Daiga: "The white man in the airport says you are not good enough for his country."

Michel joined in: "Daiga, you were too black to enter France."

Daiga grimaced. "Wait till he comes to Cameroon and we may find him too white."

They giggled as they waited for their luggage to come round, but the diplomat beside them was not amused. "Cut out the banter," he told them in a clipped tone that to Daiga sounded like a rebuke he would gladly accept. "You are in a foreign country now and you must respect its laws and customs. No more nonsense with racist tones. You are Cameroonians. They are Parisians. Act responsibly or I will send you back home!"

Orly Airport was as crowded as a town vegetable market back in Cameroon and Daiga wondered how anyone could find anyone or any place. There were airport passengers of different races pushing and dragging luggage trolleys in and out of different arrival halls and shops of all kinds. What struck Daiga was that as far as he could see blacks and Arabs almost outnumbered other races. A few wore old and worn clothes while others he thought might have been police, customs officers or even firefighters. Some were awkwardly sleeping on benches located in front of huge windows. Others sat reading newspapers and drinking coffee. Two were having their shoes polished by a black man. Even well dressed passengers seemed to roam around seeking the welcome he had been belatedly given.

Some of the students exchanged their Cameroonian money for French francs but Daiga was too spellbound at the sights and sounds of the airport to do so.

He thought that there would have been Cameroon embassy cars to transport the party to a hotel, but the diplomat merely gave them the address of a youth hostel and directed them to a bus stop near the airport. He left them with bus tickets but no time and date to see him again. Before leaving he warned them to be careful with their tongues and not refer to people they saw as black or white. "Go well to your final destinations," he finally said disappearing into the gloom of a cold Paris evening.

The students all wore suits and immediately out of the airport hallway had been taken aback by the biting cold as they were by the diplomat's disappearance from what was a grey area of the city.

"I thought this was the City of Light," Daiga said critically. "Was that not what she said in the plane before we landed?"

The cold, rendering their hands and legs numb, told them that their suits were not going to be a warm enough protection against winter in Europe. Most of them had declined to buy warm winter clothes such as greatcoats because they had planned to keep their money to purchase more valuable articles to eventually take back to Africa. They boarded the designated bus to Porte d'Italie as directed. From there the Metro took them near to their destination of Boulevard Concord Konrad Adenauer and with difficulty they found their designated youth hostel.

Chapter 2

HER LOVER'S PROMISE

Mungwi had been forlorn the whole time since she saw Daiga take off from the Douala airport. It was her first experience of an airport and it had looked to her as though Daiga was being taken to heaven never to return.

"Are you sick madam or has your husband just left you?" the cab driver asked her as they drove to the bus station for onward connection.

"No," she replied, wishing she had sat in the back seat rather than beside him in the front.

"Why have you been crying then?"

"I have not, thank you," she lied to cover Daiga's absence weighing heavily in her heart. In fact she had been haunted by a morbid thought as she watched the plane take off. The Boeing 747 of Cameroon Airlines had run for so long a time on the runway that she had feared it would not rise into the sky. She had breathed deeply with mixed relief the conditioned airport air when it rose to what she regarded as the heavens. She thought the next thing she would hear would be that the plane had crashed and Daiga killed. She winced when the cab driver asked after her health. His next question worried her more.

"If your husband has gone off to the white man's land and left you I would understand. Is that it?" The taxi driver persisted in getting near to the truth.

Even if Daiga arrived in Europe safely she thought of a worse result. They had been informally engaged for three years and, as she thought, set for marriage. Both sets of parents had long recognized the attachment and were taken aback by Daiga's departure for Europe. Friends and relations were surprised. Daiga was soon seen locally as unpredictable, ambitious and seeking adventure abroad rather than studies. What would happen to Mungwi if in Europe he found a white girl? She ignored the taxi driver's penetrating question but he persisted.

"Well, darling, if he has left you there are other men that would be glad to console you." The taxi driver broke into her thoughts with even more intrusive words she did not welcome. She reprimanded him: "My name is not darling. No more silly talk. Just drive me to the bus station or drop me and I will get another taxi!"

She pondered over what Daiga had said at the airport: "Darling, have confidence in me. I shall come back after my nine-month language course to take your hand in love and marriage." He had pledged this along with a goodbye kiss that had melted her aching heart. But this taking her hand promise had not consoled her. She was of the opinion a lover's promise often was no better than a politician's oath or a taxi driver's banter.

One thing bothered her most of all. Daiga was handsome and youthful. Any fair lady's man was he. And she knew there were many fair ladies in Germany. He was fitted for romance and she knew girls might steal him from her at first sight. That problem she already had faced at home when he had transgressed their relationship. What little she knew from wild stories about Europe made her fear worse might happen over there. One thing she was sure of was that Daiga would not remain without a white girl for his whole time in Europe. It went without saying that few single African men went to Europe without trying to date as many white girls as possibly to embroider stories for the boys back home if ever they came home. If Daiga did so the worst for her could happen. He could really fall in love and bring a white girl home to Cameroon as his wife or he could remain in Europe and never return again as she knew some Africans had done. She would have no chance of his love, or him of hers, faced with such an eventuality. Her only hope was that he might realize that he was not really single. In his words at the airport he was promised to her. Another tear dropped and this time she caught it with the back of her hand before the impertinent taxi driver sitting beside her could see it run down her cheek.

"Why would any man leave you?" the driver asked eyeing from his cab her lithesome features from head to toe as he dropped her at the bus station where she glared back at him and paid for the ride.

Back home that night she wrote Daiga a letter to keep aside until she received his address and could mail it. *"Love, I know you will never stay true when seeing those white girls. Be free to go out with them but tell them that you have your woman in Cameroon you promised to come back to. Please kindly tell the one sitting near you now that you are taken. Then read this letter to her and tell her that you love me."*

Chapter 3

NIGHTMARE IN PARIS

The students dragged their luggage out of the Metro and into the hostel yard on Boulevard Adenauer. They had debated here and there on which street to take for there were numerous side roads. Their next problem had been to trace the hostel street number. "Why did our man call it a youth hostel rather than a hotel?" asked Daiga on the way.

"It might be a type of dormitory where you have more than one person in a room," said Maria sensibly.

"That would be rubbish," Jaguar said. "We should have been put up in a hotel."

Really, however, the hostel was set up just as Maria had predicted.

The Cameroon diplomat had sent them to a youth hostel because it was cheap and their stay brief. As they entered the hostel yard carrying their luggage, they noticed it was busy with youths of different races. Asians, white and black people like themselves, were dragging luggage in and out coming or going. Like Daiga and company some had just arrived in transit or semi-permanently. The students presented themselves at the hostel desk. "*Ghihampaze,*" the receptionist exclaimed in a word and turned off to serve others. Neither of the party understood what she meant.

Jaguar asked the question they all had on their minds. "What did she say?"

"I haven't a clue," said Maria. "She does not speak like a Cameroonian."

"Of course not, That is the French you have come to learn. Speak it to them here and tell them I am a student of German not here for French."

"Pardon me, s'il vous plait," Jaguar pleaded.

"Ghihampaze les fiches," the receptionist reiterated.

"Did you get it this time?" Daiga asked Maria.

"Not a word, she seems to have breathed aloud through her nose and used a slang term. She speaks so rapidly one cannot tell the difference between her and popcorn."

"Speak to her in proper French," Daiga suggested. "This is a challenge to those of you who have come to practise French. To be taken off your feet by the first speaker is like a cripple's sport."

"Over to you."

"Okay."

"Qu'est-ce que vous avez dit, s'il vous plait?"

"Merde! Rem-plis-sez les fiches." She spoke this time slowly, more articulately, and she pointed to the forms.

"Okay," chorused the students.

"Is there any reason why she should talk through her nose?" asked Daiga with a sneer.

"That is their accent, I suppose. Let us just be polite," said Maria curtly.

They filled their forms in and presented them to the girl.

"Payez cent francs," she told Daiga, who had presented his form first. Due to the delay and detention at the airport Daiga suddenly realized he had not exchanged his Cameroonian currency. The others had done so. Hopefully, he removed a coin of the CFA zone and presented it to the girl who looked at him in surprise.

"You crazy?" the girl asked. "Crazy, you!" she repeated reversing the words to make her meaning clear.

"I am not!" Daiga exclaimed indignantly.

"You are!" the girl said sliding the coin back at him.

"I am not crazy. You talk rubbish."

"What is all this about?" Maria demanded. "Oh, Daiga, you can't pay in France with Cameroonian coins. You should have changed your Cameroonian money at the airport."

"Yes, I know that now. Remember though that you had more time to deal with the airport bank than I had."

The receptionist ignored him and continued registering other hostellers.

"Prenez salle No. 4, lit 3... merci. Salle 8, lit 5...merci..." All Daiga's mates were registered but not him. They left for their rooms leaving Daiga behind more tired than ever at what had transpired.

"This is all bullshit," he declared to himself. "I should have asked Maria for a loan. How can my first few hours in Europe be so rough? Downright nonsense is this!" He turned again to the receptionist: "Where do I exchange my Cameroonian money?"

"Down the avenue you turn right, walk forward about 150 metres. Left at Rue Bonaparte you move to house 35. There you will see the money exchange you are searching for if it is still open."

Having directed him she turned away leaving Daiga confused at the way she had rattled things off the top of her head and through her nose. She had given him directions at far too high a speed for his liking and worse she was clearly feeling her directions had satisfied him. Daiga did not want to stand there brooding like a trapped mouse. He had at least understood the first line of her spiel as being *down the avenue you turn right,* and maybe the second line, *150 metres then left at Rue Bonaparte.*

He left the youth hostel to go down the avenue turning right as instructed. He had been told to move 150 metres. How could one estimate 150 metres without a measuring device? He was shivering and his teeth vibrating with the cold. Oncoming couples clinging to their partners moved one way or the other on the sidewalk.

After a quick march of what he thought was 150 metres he started searching for the turn into Rue Bonaparte. The trouble was that he found himself on a focal point of several roads. On his right alone were three roads and they all looked the same. Which, then, was Rue Bonaparte? Had he turned left instead of right coming out of the youth hostel?

The first idea that came to his confused mind was to try the first avenue so he branched off and walked what he thought was 150 metres searching for house number 35. He saw house number 60 in a row of descending numbers, but further than that the avenue merged into one busy road by the name of Rue General Leclerc.

"I say this is rubbish the hostel woman told me," he said to himself retracing his steps. Back at the road juncture he was so confused he could not even recognize the street he had taken. He crossed straight, got lost, returned, tried another street and still was lost. He realized he urgently needed help.

"S'il vous plait. Je suis perdue!" He tried desperately to stop a hurrying man, but the man dodged nimbly past him without a word. He tried another male pedestrian who halted then, Daiga thought, looked at him as contemptuously as a white man viewing an inferior black man, sneered, and made off.

He decided to try an oncoming white woman. "S'il vous plait!" he called to one who just smiled and hardly paused. "Being in France is like bathing in trash," he grumbled to himself before fixing on another female figure coming from the opposite direction. "If force is required to find my way I will use it," he determined thinking he was down to his last resource of politeness.

"S'il vous plait!" he called out when the girl was a few metres in front. She did not answer. He called s'il vous plaît again. The girl ignored him and swerved aside to pass.

"C'est à toi que je parle," he asserted, attempting to grip the girl's hand, but she again swerved to avoid him. "Merde, qu'est qui t'arrive?" she demanded of him.

"Where is Rue Bonaparte?" he asked pointedly noticing how lovely she looked even in the semi dark.

"I don't know," she replied, retreating backwards to keep away from him. "Let me pass."

"You must know! That is why I seek your help."

""I tell you I don't know," she insisted trying to force her way. Daiga caught hold of her clumsily by the dress below her open coat. "I need help. I tell you that if you don't help me you don't go. I am a stranger lost in this big city. It is your duty to help me."

Other pedestrians hurried past them fearful of interfering in a couple's disagreement. A glance was more than enough before each made off.

"I arrived from Cameroon only today and need to change my money but I don't know where the exchange house is. You are here in Paris and surely must know the street with such a prominent name as Rue Bonaparte."

"Not everyone in Paris knows everywhere. If you don't know yourself you need take a taxi and it will drop you there. In the meantime let go of my dress, monsieur, or I warn you I will scream for help!"

"No need for that. No need for a taxi. How would I pay? I need French francs in exchange for my Cameroon money. I was told the exchange office is not far from this street on Rue Bonaparte."

"Keep looking for the exchange and let me go!" she exclaimed still trying to free herself. "Leave me alone or I will call for the police."

"You are not going until you help me!" Daiga insisted not knowing that his antics were being watched. Two policemen crossed the road and closed in on him grabbing each arm.

"You dare harass this woman," one barked out before letting go. "Show us your passport identifying yourself, monsieur, or let us see your permit to be in France."

"I do not have it," Daiga said as the girl slipped away without even the policemen knowing. From where had the officers arrived? Daiga recalled being told that French agents de police were omnipresent and that they were biased against black men.

"What identification documents do you have then?"

"I do not have them here."

"You may be an alien here in France."

"I am not! I arrived from Cameroon today and I shall be lodging at the youth hostel on rue Conrad Adenauer. I left my passport in my box there and was intending to change Cameroonian currency into French currency to pay the hostel receptionist who gave me directions to currency exchange."

"Searching for a currency exchange at this time of night? Search him!" the sergeant ordered his colleague. The policeman found Daiga's one hundred thousand Cameroonian francs and his airline ticket to West Germany. "Where is your passport and what is your name?"

''It is with my luggage. I am Foncham Daiga."

"And where is your luggage?"

"I told you that it is at the youth hostel on Conrad Adenauer."

One of the agents consulted a handbook and wrote down a telephone number. Then they all moved to a nearby telephone booth where he dialed the number. Daiga could clearly hear voices as the person at the desk gave his name.

"Police!" the officer announced. "Has anyone by name of Foncham Daiga booked to spend the night at your hostel?"

"One moment. What was the name?"

This was not the female voice Daiga had expected. It was a man's voice asking for his name.

"Foncham Daiga. Wait a minute and I will spell it for you." The policeman then asked Daiga to spell his name and he repeated it on the phone.

"No sir," was the blunt reply.

"Hold the line please for a moment."

Daiga had interrupted the conversation. "I did not say I had booked in. I was trying to book in," he told the policeman. "My Cameroon money was unchanged as you can see. I had to go and make an exchange and the hostel receptionist was a woman, not this man you are talking to. She told me how to get to the money exchange. She gave me lousy directions and I got lost. I was asking the woman for directions. My box with my documents is in the reception hall at the youth hostel."

"What is the colour of your box?"

"Red."

The officer picked up the phone again. "Look around the hall please and see if there is a red box." The phone went dead for about 20 seconds and clicked alive when the man from the other end spoke.

"I see no red box here, sir."

"You are sure."

"Yes."

There was silence for a minute before the policeman hung up.

He turned on Daiga saying: "You must be telling lies. Are you an illegal resident here in France?" He drew Daiga's hands behind him and quickly fitted handcuffs amid his protests.

"I am not illegal. I just arrived from Douala for a course in German in Stuttgart. Why are you doing this?"

"Well, we will see about your course in Stuttgart."

"He may be nuts. Let's take him in," the other policeman urged his colleague.

The officer spoke into his walkie-talkie and in less than seven minutes a police van arrived and Daiga was pushed in. It was 10 o'clock when they arrived at the Station of the 23rd District of the Mobile Intervention Police. Daiga was given a seat in the superintendent's office and his cuffs were hooked to his chair. There were other men and women of African and Asian origin also cuffed to chairs.

"We may have one more air ticket to purchase," the officer told the superintendent. "We have one more clandestine to be deported. This one is destined for Cameroon."

"What? I am not clandestine," Daiga protested. "You surely saw that I had an air ticket to Germany. I am flying there tomorrow for a language course in Stuttgart. I was sent to Germany, through France, by my government in Cameroon."

"Then we can send you on to West Germany, but without papers your chances of staying there will be zero."

"I have papers."

"Where are they now?" the superintendent asked showing a hint of the concern Daiga welcomed.

"They are in my box at the youth hostel."

"On the contrary," responded the sergeant. "We called the hostel. He is not registered there nor is the box he is talking about anywhere to be found."

"I swear that I am telling the truth, sir. We can go there and check if you really seek the truth. I assure you that we will find the box and you can talk to my fellow students."

"He does have Cameroon money and an air ticket to West Germany. We surely cannot ignore that. I really think you should check this out more fully sergeant. Why don't you drive him down to the youth hostel and find out if he is known to anyone there? He says he came with a party of students. It won't cost you a weekend, just 20 or so minutes."

The sergeant and constable escorted Daiga back to the van and they drove to the hostel. It was midnight by the time they arrived. The receptionist Daiga had dealt with had long since gone home. She had left an hour ago her nightshift replacement told them. It was he who had received the police call and explained he had not seen Daiga's box.

"My classmates will identify me," Daiga confidently told the police officer.

"Will they?"

"My mates journeyed with me from Cameroon today and they are here. Seven of them are now in their beds. I can give you their names. You can interview them."

"What are their names?"

Daiga recited the names and the registrar found them to be correct. "Yes, the names are listed with rooms and beds," he told the police officers. "But they must be asleep now."

"Waken them. Call them down here," ordered the officer. The night watch went first to waken Maria in the women's dormitory. Descending, rubbing her eyes, she winced at seeing Daiga in handcuffs.

"Daiga, what is happening to you?" she asked "What have you done?"

"Answer *me* first," the sergeant broke in. "Who is this Daiga?"

"We are classmates fresh from Douala, Cameroon, this evening for language courses. He is one of us."

"Can I see your passport and other papers?"

Maria hurried back upstairs for her papers while the officers spoke to other students who had come down. Each one identified Daiga to them. One officer asked if there was any class list and it was found and given to him. Daiga's name was there. Who had taken away Daiga's red box with all his papers in it? No one knew, but the policeman had a good idea. "Youth hostels sometimes harbour thieves. You must all be very careful with your belongings. But we still have a charge against you, monsieur. We picked you up harassing a female pedestrian."

Daiga's mates eased the tension by trying to make light of this. They had seen how women could make him do foolish things. "He would never hurt a woman," they contended on his behalf.

"Okay, you can all go back to bed now and excuse us for the disturbance," said the police sergeant before escorting Daiga back to the van. One of the officers decided to make another search for his belongings. At a distance near the end of the lobby his eyes fell on something behind a sofa.

"Wait a minute," he demanded of his colleague. It was a half-opened red box. He called Daiga back. "Is this your luggage?"

"Yes, it is!" Daiga exclaimed with a huge sigh of relief.

"Check it to see if everything is in order." Daiga rummaged around his things to find that the important thing he needed most was not there. His passport was gone but his Cameroonian identity card had been left behind. Two suits he had picked up from a shop in Douala had been taken. All his university documents were there. The officer picked them up and flipped through them.

"Where is your passport then?"

"I don't know. It has disappeared."

"This is not unusual," said the police officer. "Someone may even now be impersonating you using your passport. There are villains here whose sole business is stealing passports. I must take you to the station and establish a certificate of lost documents to enable you to continue your journey to West Germany. The German immigration police will take it up from there. You have an air ticket don't you?"

"Yes."

"Why were you harassing that young woman?"

"I needed help. I was lost and desperate for directions to the money exchange. I had almost lost my mind not knowing where I was. I was asking her for directions. She was in no danger."

"Well, maybe we can sort things out since she is not here to register a complaint and so that you can continue your journey immediately."

The police eventually listed what was lost on a certificate and Daiga, with what other of his belongings that were found, was driven to the airport in the police van. Lucky for him he arrived in time to catch the first plane to Bonn that morning.

"Thank you, sir," Daiga said to the police officer without conviction before passing through the departure gate. "That was a narrow escape for me. I will not forget my misadventure in Paris and the help of the French police."

"Don't hang your nose too much on chicks, boy?" the flattered policeman candidly advised him. "German chicks can be more dangerous than the French."

Soon Daiga was flying to Bonn but not without regrets. He had left without even the chance of a word with his classmates. His intention to send postcards to Africa from France after his first night there had not worked out either. He had thought of going to a nightclub and finding excitement with a French girl like the one he had grappled with on the street or had lousy instructions from at the youth hostel. But no such luck. His few hours in France had been rough. He felt no better than a deportee. He imagined he would be handed directly to the German police when the plane reached Bonn. He hesitated to imagine how uniformed Germans, possibly still smarting over two lost world wars, would treat a black man from Cameroon who had lost his identification documents?

Chapter 4

NIGHT OF THE NJANGI

A traditional Cameroon event popularly known as *njangi* comes up at the end of each month. Members would meet, contribute money and give it to a chosen individual to help him bring in his crops or fix up his home. The following month they would do it all again for another member's family until in a fair way they had gone round all members and added to compound prosperity.

The recipient family had to prepare food and drinks and help entertain members in his compound. The eating, drinking and dancing all night often ended in drunken misbehaviour.

This particular week it was Mungwi's Uncle Bobga to claim the windfall. Uncle Bobga was a proud businessman who never wanted his ideas to compete with those of any other person. He loved to do his things personally with distinction.

He invited his niece to assist in the epicurean preparations. The delicacies ranged from egusi pudding, bean cakes, salad, rice, parched groundnuts and crackers to plantains, pounded coco, yams and fufu. Drinks included whisky, champagne, brandy, gin, schnapps and locally brewed beer. There was usually an abundance of everything and much of it was often wasted. Food would be scattered around, drinks mixed and often vomited until the wee hours ended festivities in fond farewells or drunken brawls.

All day Mungwi and her cousins prepared food and arranged seats. She worked well but as usual she had Daiga on her mind. The last time her uncle had been honored with this ceremony Mungwi and Daiga had both enjoyed it immensely. Daiga had protected her against harassment from drunkards trying to dance with her. This time she was bound to face the attention of probably the same drunkards knowing Daiga was away.

When midnight arrived the feasting and merriment reached a climax. Stomachs were saturated with a jumble of everything. The men ran helter skelter after the ladies and danced with disequilibrium, knocking down bottles and glasses and ignoring decorum. The discotheque man picked hard rock numbers meant to make dancers jump and roll. "Now, the rollicking sounds, the midnight sounds!" cried out one dancer when a slow dance ended. A man, who had drank to capacity, dragged Mungwi to the floor as he had done a previous time.

"I am tired," she implored him and tore herself from his clumsy grasp.

"You become tired only when I want to dance with you," he said pulling her back with conflicting words.

"No! I said I was tired," she insisted and dodged the drunken man who was leaning on her. She slipped to the side and the man crashed on the wall and was so vexed he retorted: "You silly girl. You think you are preserving yourself for Daiga. Don't be mistaken. Daiga doesn't intend to come back to you from Germany. He will likely marry a white girl and continue his studies in Germany!"

The words true or false came at Mungwi like a stroke of lightning. She was momentarily devastated by what he had said and could not stop the man taking her in his arms. Luckily for both of them the rollicking sound had been replaced by a slow dance and she actually enjoyed for a short time the almost forgotten feel of a man drunk as this one truly was.

When she came round and got rid of the interloper she retreated to her sleeping room her mind preoccupied by what he had said. What had she heard? That Daiga did not intend to come back to her. This was heartbreaking. Even though the revelation came from a drunkard there could be truth to it. The man, by name Doh, was a brother of Daiga's bosom friend and student at the University of Yaounde. Had they somehow heard of Daiga's intention? There was never smoke without fire. Nor was it the first time she had heard this about Daiga. One of her friends, a girl studying at the university, had warned her of his likely goings on.

"Watch the way you rely on Daiga as a future husband. He looks like one who is coming home from Europe with a white girl," were her words. On top of being a darling to women Mungwi knew Daiga was also a proud man. Everybody knew that bringing back a white girl from Europe rarely occurred but gave real prestige when it did. It seemed everyone suspected Daiga would eventually do so for that same reason.

"I shall drop you a postcard immediately I land in Paris and before taking my transit flight," he had told Mungwi. Had he kept his promise the card would have reached Douala and taken less than a week to reach Bamenda. But a month had passed without a word from him. Was he involved with someone? Had he abandoned her? Was their relationship over?

How would she fare if Daiga had taken a white girl. Their families especially had recognized them very much as a couple. Mungwi thought her life would end if Daiga did not come back to her. Whenever she had gone to Bali she had spent most of her time in Daiga's compound. She would buy nice little things for Daiga's younger sisters and brothers. She sewed dresses for Daiga's mother and followed her to the farm whenever she could to help with the crops and hens.

Daiga had marched into her father's compound at any time day or night and led her out for a walk. He had attended ceremonies there and at Daiga's compound all his relations had come to recognize and love her. If Daiga abandoned her how would she explain it to their families? How would she behave in front of her friends if she were left high and dry on the shelf without him?

Whenever her friends had met her the thing after her health would be to ask after Daiga. For feasts and parties their invitation cards had carried the names Daiga and Mungwi.

Because Daiga would rarely let a beautiful girl pass by without eyeing her up he had risked difficult times with his impetuous nature. Mungwi had once overheard a conversation between him and a female friend of hers whom he had taken to the farm to pick vegetables and after that to his compound home.

When his amorous intentions became clear to the girl she had struggled out of his arms saying: "Please, Daiga, let me go. I really fear being here should Mungwi arrive. She would hate me for life."

"Mungwi is a girl. You are a girl. I chose her. I can also choose you," he had boldly asserted to her consternation.

"No, you have gone too far with Mungwi. So far that no one including me would take you in earnest if you were to change your love for her to me. Everyone recognizes you and Mungwi as a pair. The villagers might even threaten to cast you out of the compound. They love Mungwi. You must not betray her by playing around with me."

"Since you came here of your own free will that's funny of you to say that. The truth is that I can start a pairing with you now that others would soon recognize," insisted an indignant Daiga.

"Daiga, get this right. I can't do what you want me to do. I can't go out with you. I do not want people to curse me. I'll scream if you kiss me again. Be honest with Mungwi. Mungwi is honest with you."

On saying this the girl tore herself from him and made for the door. There she had bumped into Mungwi, who, at the inopportune moment had come visiting and had overheard some of what was said. Mungwi was apparently satisfied with her friend's response because she said hello to be met with embarrassment and a silent retreat. She entered Daiga's home saying she had overheard what was said. She would not put up with it and if it happened again he really would have to find someone else.

Daiga had begged her forgiveness swearing it would never happen again and softening her stand in his arms.

Now that Daiga was in Europe no one at home in Cameroon knew what he was doing or planning to do for his pleasure. She had lost any control she ever had over him. She feared that no one in all of Europe would know to respect her by rejecting her man like her friend had rejected him. He might line up a school of girls and chase them without thought of betrayal. He would know that she would never know for certain what he was doing until he himself told her at home in Cameroon that he still loved her as she loved him.

The Njangi party that night had left Mungwi feeling downcast at what she had heard and undecided what she could do about her pitifully lovelorn state of body and mind.

Chapter 5

GERMAN WENCHES

Daiga was the only black person in the West German Lufthansa Boeing 737 headed for Bonn. The rest were whites with a considerable number of Asians. For the first time in his life Daiga felt an inferiority complex in the midst of people. Luckily he felt well dressed in his superior woolen suit while the others were mostly casually dressed.

After about half an hour's time in the air, the hostess came round asking passengers if they would like to eat or drink. Daiga thought the hostess gave him special attention. Her smile seemed broader and more concerned with his well being.

"Would you like something?" the charming German woman he judged was about 23 years of age asked him.

"Yes, please," Daiga answered smiling back at her.

"A soft drink or a beer?"

"Beer, for me, of course."

The hostess pulled the trolley right up to him and served him then wished him a good appetite.

"Thanks very much," he winked her as food and drink were placed on the lowered wooden carrier before him.

He listened to hear if she wished good appetite to the other passengers but they spoke in a detailed German that Daiga did not understand. The meal was typical. It consisted of potatoes churned in cabbage soup and pork. As he ate he thought how nice it would be to make contact with this particular hostess, but when he remembered that in Bonn he would be handed directly to police he cast the thought from his mind.

"Put your nose off the German chicks," he remembered the French police officer telling him. "Chicks can be funny." Or was it that they could be dangerous? He tried to remember the exact spoken words. No woman would be funny with him and get away with it. No woman in Africa ever had done so. Nor would they even try any funny tricks in Cameroon where men ruled the roost. Yet, he was already learning this might not always be the case in Europe and it troubled him. There were cultural differences he had best be aware of. The dangerous people would be the German police and he was likely to land directly in their hands in Bonn. The cute hostess might even see police arrest him at the airport. Maybe he would be handcuffed and driven in a police van to the station for questioning as had happened in Paris.

He finished eating and took hold of his can of beer. He wondered why they were serving Dutch Heineken in Germany. He grasped the clip and drew it off quickly without paying attention. There was an explosion and beer squirted out wetting his clothes and those of two passengers seated to his left.

"I am so sorry. Excuse me," he apologized. The two picked up the napkins on their trays and tried to wipe the liquid off their clothes.

"I never knew this can was going to explode on us."

"Niggers never do know anything," retorted one of the two passengers. After saying this he signaled to the hostess who had served them and suggested he change his seat for another.

Daiga had read in books that blacks were openly called niggers in America by some racist whites but he had never been addressed that way himself. This fellow had callously called him nigger right to his face. He could not let the insult go unchallenged. Such an uncouth person would hear his piece of retaliation.

"I thought I apologized you white monkey?" Daiga exclaimed back at the passenger by then up on his feet again asking the hostess for an empty seat away from Daiga in the middle row of the plane.

"Sorry, sorry!" exclaimed the hostess on seeing the mess. She hurried to the front of the plane then came back with a cloth to wipe up the spilt alcohol.

"Sorry, indeed," she lamented as though she was the cause. She cleared away Daiga's tray and packed it on top of other trays on her trolley. Then she wiped his suit down to his waist. As she pushed the trolley past the two other passengers she apologized to them too and wiped their suits.

"Please don't be angered by a simple accident of spilt beer."

Daiga was touched by her humble attitude and hoped all German women would have the same attribute. In contrast to her sympathy he felt that the white passengers were looking at him contemptuously and even with scorn. He, too, had a wet suit from his accidentally spilt beer. There were even traces of beer on his face and hair. He took out a handkerchief and cleaned himself further. When the hostess brought another napkin for him he waved her off saying there was no more need of it but he gladly accepted the fresh can of beer she brought and her gesture in safely opening it for him.

"Anger was not my intent," he said cooling down. "Please take another apology from me to those two gentlemen."

A jerk of the plane was followed by the click of a bell and the melodious voice of a stewardess announcing first in German then in English and French: "Ladies and gentlemen, we are now descending on Bonn, where the time is 3.15 a.m. and the temperature six degrees centigrade. Kindly extinguish cigarettes, fasten seatbelts and remain seated."

A wave of apprehension seized Daiga. How would he be treated on landing? He had neither passport nor anything that would clear him through immigration. He looked out of the window on the city below. It had thousands of lights and from high in the air he detected streets and avenues shimmering in streaks of light and darkness. Lights circled the city twice and he saw it as large and mysterious. What he imagined down there were a few big hotels or nightclubs bright with neon signs. Had his papers been in order and evening at hand he probably would have picked up a cab after landing and gone to one of the hotels for a night. After a warm bath he imagined he would have visited a nightclub and picked up feminine company. If unsuccessful at a nightclub a brothel would have done if such things existed in Germany. But heavy on his mind was the fact that his papers were not in order and the reality that his plane was about to land in the middle of the morning.

Soon the plane hissed and the wheels screeched on the tarmac. Daiga looked out as it taxied to a stop off the runway for final disembarkation. When the plane came to a halt the passengers started crowding down the aisle. Daiga lowered his hand luggage from the upper bin but his mind was full of dire thoughts of the unknown as he followed the others out. He smiled to the stewardess but there were numerous questions swirling around in his head. What was going to happen to him? What would the immigration officers do to him this time? Even if released from the airport how would he act if accosted by police? His mind was charged with these questions on his way to the arrival desk. What happened to Daiga at the desk was like a minor miracle he thought accomplished by God.

The desk officer asked first in German then in decent English, "Your passport please." Before Daiga could gabble out his full story the officer broke in: "Are you by any chance Daiga from Cameroon?"

Overwhelmed and shivering with fright, Daiga managed to say yes.

"Your paper, please." The officer stretched out a hand.

"I have none."

"I mean your attestation of lost documents."

Daiga managed to react though not knowing how this airport man had come to know about his loss of documents.

"Have a seat please. Sorry for your mishaps in France. We sent a telegram to your embassy. Someone is going to be here shortly to take care of you and prepare a new passport. You look tired. Take a rest."

Daiga could not believe the efficiency and thoughtfulness. Was it all that easy even at this time of the morning? He had feared deportation back to Cameroon for he had heard stories of the way German police acted with suspected illegal immigrants. This flashed through his mind even though he was not immigrating and certainly not illegally. He decided on the spot that it might be that critics had mistaken hardihood and resolve for harsh wickedness in the German people. He had read about World War II German audacity to the point of foolishly fighting Russia right into Moscow then retreating in defeat through winter snow and ice back to Germany and this picture too flashed through his mind as he watched not German soldiers but airport workers efficiently carry out their duties. When he closed his tired eyes he wondered what Mungwi was doing back home in Cameroon. He had no idea that words shaping their future were troubling her during sleepless nights.

He dreamed of being home with Mungwi, away from France and Germany, and the dangers that might lie ahead.

Someone tapped his shoulder startling him and wakening him and telling him he would escort him through the gate into the reception hall. To Daiga the hall looked rather like a huge snack and entertainment bar, taking into account the discotheque stands, television and video screens, cafeteria and even video games. Groups of passengers were watching the different screens; others were eating and drinking; still others slept on sofas or nodded in chairs. The hall smelled clean and classy to him. He bought a hamburger and a pastry, then a can of apple juice and sat down to appreciate a one-man German musical show even at that time in the morning. The area where he sat was cosmopolitan and comfortable. This was like the Europe he had dreamed of visiting and his usual confidence returned. Things were simply suddenly looking up for Daiga.

After 10 minutes a loudspeaker broke out with a message and Daiga heard his name announced. "Mr. Foncham Daiga, passenger from Cameroon, is expected at the information desk," the announcement repeated first in German then English and French. Daiga did present himself at the desk and was introduced to a young man of about 30 who spoke better English than did he.

"Are you Daiga Foncham?"

"Yes sir."

"I am the cultural attaché at the Cameroon Embassy here. I was telephoned to come and pick you up."

"Thank you very much. Sorry to bother you so early in the morning."

"We had been expecting you tomorrow, but that's okay."

"I decided to make a stopover in Paris after my flight from Cameroon, but landed in difficulties and had to come early."

"Yes, we learned of your troubles."

The man escorted him out of the airport to a parking lot with an airport aide carrying his luggage to the trunk of an Opel. The attaché tossed a mark to the aide. Daiga was impressed. The man also spoke French with a Cameroonian accent as they discussed Bamenda, Douala and Yaounde. He was happy to see a Cameroonian civil servant doing his job with hospitality and kindness. This was not his experience of Cameroonian civil servants at home.

"Okay, Mr. Daiga," said the diplomat. "After you briefly freshen up at the embassy, I shall drop you at a hostel where you will spend the rest of what is left of the night. Tomorrow I will provide you with a passport and a railway warrant to Stuttgart. You will also receive your allowance. You don't have to come too early. Here's my card. Okay?"

"Thank you, sir." Daiga replied feeling at home with the diplomat but not looking forward to another hostel. Things were not going to be as rough as he had feared though. He would soon have a passport and the next day travel by train to Stuttgart to start his education in German. After half an hour at the embassy, which proved to be the diplomat's home, Daiga was driven to the Mission Youth Hostel where he did sleep for a few hours and to his relief without trouble. The next morning he easily found the right bus to drop him back at the address of the Cameroon Embassy given to him by the cultural attaché. The German buses were efficient and punctual. On arrival, he was given a passport decently written out and with the photograph he had provided professionally attached.

"You now have your passport and this is your bursary package of deutschmarks for the month of November. Your December allowance will be mailed to your university. You should now go by rail to Stuttgart. The university administration knows you are coming. Here is your rail warrant and the time of your train. You will be responsible for the rest of the arrangements for your German language course and residence. Be careful with your papers and your money. Some people here are not very different from those I heard you encountered in France. Housing is not difficult in Stuttgart especially for foreign students. You may get a university room and that will be less expensive and socially better for study and learning. Be as independent as possible of the embassy for we don't have time to attend personally to you. Privately, for your information, we contract marriages. Handsome unmarried guys like you can always pick up a German frâulien, who would help you learn German quicker and make your stay independent of the embassy. There is still a shortage of men in Germany. We willingly contract marriages!" That said, he winked, tapped Daiga lightly on the shoulder, and accompanied him to a bus stop for transport to the Bonn passenger train station.

Daiga left the embassy feeling on top of the world and wondering if the diplomat was joking about marriages. He had a passport, money for a month without converting his own money and more money promised the following month. Now he could play his hand independently. At the train station he kept his luggage close by and after presenting his railway warrant took the only vacant train seat beside an older woman he thought of as a German hag and soon found out she spoke only her German language.

"Guten morgen!" the woman greeted Daiga, who responded with a few token words in German.

She said something else in German that he did not understand since the level of his German was hardly beyond the greeting stage. He nodded and turned his head to the window so as not to be embarrassed any further. The electric express train swept past forests, tunnels, hills, animals villages and people charging at him like Allied troops had charged Germans and vice versa in World War II's battle of the Rhine. He saw remnants of a war that had ended some 25 years previously.

To Daiga this really was becoming a modern world a hundred years ahead of Africa. He wondered how the victorious European countries had progressed compared with the loser. He wished his schoolmates back in Bambili could see him in an electric train running smoothly on time at 100 kilometres an hour. The woman beside him again asked something he did not understand. He just nodded. She opened her bag and instead of words brought out an apple for him.

"Danke," he said appreciating her spontaneous generosity.

A half hour later the woman handed him a fresh banana. He was less generous in speech this time. "Even the best bananas from Africa are sent to these white monkeys and the rotten ones left for us to put worms in our stomachs. What a world!" he moaned to her, not in English or French, but in his native tongue that he knew she would not understand and might quiet her. The woman smiled fully perplexed. Daiga wished she were younger. He thought he would have tried an adventure with her except that she was so old there would be no difference in bed between her and a plantain sucker. She further bored him by constantly smiling and tapping him on the shoulder to look at vines that in autumn would bear grapes for Stuttgart's famous wines. Another tap came for him to view the Neckar River. When they reached the Stuttgart railway station, the woman invited Daiga for coffee. He turned down the invitation but he carried both her light luggage and his heavier cases out from the train.

He found baggage carts for the two of them for their luggage and strolling together on their way they passed a wine shop. "Here is money," she told him. "Buy me that bottle of wine up there on the top shelf inside the window."

Daiga did so although the shopkeeper had to use a ladder and pinchers to bring down the bottle. She invited him for a glass of wine as her guest at her place but he again declined. "Danke," she said politely as he was leaving her to go by cab to the university hostel. "Here, take my card if some other time you would like to join me. I live not too far from your university."

Daiga placed the card in his yellow pouch hanging around his neck for safety and waved her goodbye. As his taxi took off his thoughts told him he would not be visiting her.

At the university Daiga was designated a student room in block D ninth floor. There were about 30 students, male and female, quartered on the same floor. They shared two common kitchens and a big lounge where they could meet and watch television. Television was new to Daiga. *The Bionic Woman,* a current American hit show in Germany, roused his senses, as did what he thought of as bionic female German students sharing the lounge with him. His time would come with them he assured himself as they cast fleeting glances at him without speaking he was glad to find.

His mind, adrift between the female students and Lindsay Wagner's dubbed language skills on the television screen, gave Daiga little understanding of the spin-off from the *Die Sieben Millionen Dollar Frau* as it was known in Germany. He sat goggle-eyed watching the antics of what he considered pure magic right there before his eyes as the episode *Dead Ringer* unwound.

Daiga was the only black student on the floor and one of few at the university. Lucky for him the university's language laboratory was in the basement of the same building as his bedroom so he did not have to cross the campus for classes. This meant he could spend much of his time in the laboratory even until midnight each night. The university restaurant was close by too. So was the swimming pool to help him exercise and admire women in stylish bikinis. Ease of access helped him study without interruption except by thoughts of conquest whenever a female approached. Daiga, a constant admirer of women, was handicapped in seduction because he spoke German so poorly. This made him aware of a complex in front of girls. When, in conversation, he faced the embarrassment of his German phrases being corrected time and again and his errors in grammar occasionally thrown back at him with background giggles, he backed away.

His principal teacher was a woman who always seemed to give lessons on German food when he was ravenously hungry. A few British, Dutch, and Danish students studied alongside him and close by were a thousand German students busy with other subjects. Being almost the only black student at times set him apart but there was no real discrimination that he was aware of and he gradually began to assert himself.

Daiga was a proud man so his lack of fluent German turned out to be soul destroying in keeping him apart from his fair-haired contemporaries during the first few weeks at university. Yet he saw that this actually was helping him master what he was soon to himself call his future language of conquest. His keenness to socialize and exchange words with females helped him work harder at his German studies. Within two months he had polished his German and was able to read the *Stuttgart Zeitung* newspaper and converse hesitantly if not fairly well with his professor and with Germans generally.

Time was flying by fast though and he did not welcome the prospect of leaving Stuttgart and the good things he was experiencing at university and down town where beer and wine was so good and women so beautiful.

Chapter 6

SEMESTER OF DISCONTENT

Knowing his government allowance and language classes would be ending weighed heavily on Daiga's mind as the months passing by turned to weeks of growing concern.

He knocked on the door of the student council office to talk over his difficulties first with the council secretary who introduced him to the president. "I need financial help to complete my studies since my allowance from my government is ending soon. Can you help me?"

"There is not much we can do," said Wolfgang Reuter, quickly indicating that Daiga was wasting his time. "Were you *supposed* to stay in Germany more than a year? You cannot expect the state or college students to subsidize you. I consider you have two options. The first is to return to your homeland to avoid difficulties with the German immigration authorities and, secondly, if by some chance you convince them to give you more time in Germany do what other students do. Get a night job."

"I agree," Daiga replied. "Since you suggest work, where do I find work?"

"Well, right under your nose for one place. I know that the student bar directly below us continually needs bar servers. They don't pay much, but you might earn tips to tide you over. See the bar boss downstairs. Or try to get an interview with the company owner. I warn you though. If you get a job don't do what one server was doing. He was drinking as much beer as he served. So, there may be a vacancy."

Daiga took the student council president's prudent advice and just a day later he was behind the bar serving beer to fellow students. The tips were few and far between and the pay was, as he was warned, poor. One night, after working at the bar, he examined his situation while carefully turning out pockets and his yellow pouch to count his money. Out with the cash and onto his bed from his pouch fell a card he had forgotten all about. He picked it up apprehensively. "Oh, yes," he remembered the card was given him by the friendly old German lady on the train seven months previous when he had first arrived in Stuttgart.. He recalled that she had invited him to visit her and that she lived fairly close to the university. He conjured with the idea of going to find out if she could put him up with lodgings in her home to help his finances. He had her name and address in front of him. She was old and might need home help or security herself that he could supply in return for accommodation. It would mean giving up his university apartment. Necessity governed his next action of knocking at the door of Frau Gertrude Braun.

If Daiga had expected a welcome he was not disappointed. Frau Braun recognized him and invited him into her living room. Daiga found she was not alone in the house. She had a pretty young niece with her. The girl was of little more than 17 years of age. Gertrude introduced them: "Marlene meet… ah, I forget your name."

"I am Daiga, from Cameroon."

"Yes, of course, so, Marlene, meet Daiga. Now I remember. We shared two seats beside each other on a train almost a year ago and I recall him helping me with my luggage and buying me a bottle of wine."

Daiga turned to the young girl flashing a smile and saying: "Hello! How are you? Don't you have school today?"

"I have this afternoon off."

Marlene did not say another word as Daiga and Gertrude recalled their experiences meeting on the train. Marlene watched him closely though and he asked her if she had ever traveled by train. "Of course I have," she replied simply staring at him so seemingly embarrassed that Daiga stopped trying to draw her out and turned again to her aunt.

"You have a wonderful country here and a wonderful city," was all he could think of saying. "The university is excellent. If I were to meet a woman I loved I would settle down here."

"Well, there are plenty unmarried German women to choose from," the old lady encouraged him. "But don't go running after my niece. She is too young for you."

"Of course not," Daiga responded, himself embarrassed by her blunt talk and lacking the courage to look straight at Marlene was lost for further words.

Gertrude laughed at his plight.

Gertrude suggested Marlene brew up tea and they would share it with cake, Marlene immediately walked the few steps to the kitchen. Daiga heard her fill the kettle and light the ring.

"Marlene is still at high school," Gertrude said. "So what brings you here, Daiga?"

Daiga had to think fast. He was realizing that he could not tell Gertrude his true intention. It would have been too much of a sudden intrusion. "It is an overdue social call," he simply said, hiding his financial difficulties and need of help.

"There must be more to it than just a social call after nearly a year. Stuttgart is a big city. I'm surprised you found me."

"You gave me your calling card and invited me to your home before we parted at the railway station."

"Now I remember. You were so helpful with my luggage."

Marlene interrupted the conversation returning from the kitchen with a loaded tea tray. Tea for three followed and a marble cake was enjoyed after Gertrude had filled their cups.

"You can't possibly know but I am here at Stuttgart University from Cameroon, in West Africa, learning German," Daiga said direct to Marlene to again try to draw her out. She smiled eyes downcast but saying not a word and leading him to think that she probably did not know where West Africa was let alone Cameroon.

"I would think you may be going to university soon," he continued. "If you wish I could show you around if your aunt would permit me. I am free on Saturday afternoon if you should be free too."

Marlene suddenly showed she had a mind of her own. Without consulting her aunt, she surprised him in replying: "Then I will meet you at the university cafeteria at 2 p.m. I would like to see the facilities."

Her aunt's eyes opened wide but she nodded her permission. To her Daiga seemed a nice young man black or white. "That would free me to do some shopping alone."

Daiga was feeling more and more out of place before the last cake crumbs had disappeared. He was soon embarrassed by silence around the table and ready to leave an old woman and a young girl he still had little in common with except to know that she was young and attractive and he had a date with her. He rose a bit regretting having come to Gertrude's home in the first place and he feared the situation might change to his disadvantage if he stayed too long. "Well, it was nice meeting you again. Thanks for tea," he politely addressed the old lady before turning to Marlene. "I'm looking forward to seeing you again. I have a university class late this afternoon but I will be happy to show you around on Saturday."

With that he turned on his heels no doubt leaving his hostess concerned and bewildered and he thinking that by cultivating her niece if she turned up he might find cheap or free lodgings to tide him over during further studies if worse came to worst.

Chapter 7

STRUDEL FOR TWO

Saturday had been a long time coming, Daiga thought, as he waited impatiently for the cafeteria clock hands to reach 2 o'clock.

He acted surprised when Marlene strolled through the doorway and up to his table right on time. "I never imagined you would come," he bid welcome. "Would you like a coffee and cake?"

"A strawberry strudel would be nice," she replied on inspecting the display at the counter.

"Okay, strudel it is," Daiga agreed with a grin. "It's tea and strudel for two."

Daiga was impressed with the smart purple twin-suit she wore but he felt unusually guilty at realizing how young she looked and how a smudge of lipstick accentuated her fair hair above a lovely face and longish neck that he had failed to appreciate before.

He sat down smiling earnestly into her blue eyes after serving the table. He foolishly said he had never seen such eyes in all his days in Africa.

She was not taken in by his flattery. "There are blue eyes all over this cafeteria," she smiled back at him. "German eyes usually are blue just as African eyes are often brown."

"Very perceptive," he acknowledged though a bit taken aback. "I was talking about the almost black eyes of Africa. Eyes like mine."

Daiga averted his gaze realizing flattery with this fraulein would likely get him nowhere. "Did your aunt ask about our date?" he questioned her. "You should have brought her with you. She warned you about me."

"I assured her our date was nothing more than to tour the university. I hope to enroll here in a year to study music and art. In any case she has other things to do this afternoon. Being here gives her a break from me and me a break from the piano and furthermore a chance to practise my English."

"Your English, Marlene, is excellent."

"That's because my father was an Englishman and saw to it that I studied for a time in England."

"At high school?"

"At a private school in London."

"Your father must have been resourceful."

"I'm not so sure of that. If you are talking about his financial side he went bankrupt before his death."

"Ah! So sorry. You seem to have taken it well. I ask too much personal stuff. Forgive me."

"Yes, you tend to."

"Well, my African musical background probably would not suit the piano and my English actually is not as good as yours. I have some records in my room you might enjoy. We have great musicians and singers in Africa. A very lovely love song is Malaika; the words are something like…I will sing them softly... *Malaika, you're my angel Malaika, you're the girl of my dreams, the one I adore…"*

"It's lovely--but stop. You embarrass me. If my aunt knew I was sitting with you listening to you sing a romantic ballad she would be justly concerned. You promised to show me around the university. I have only crispy crumbs left of my delicious strawberry strudel and I thank you for it. Shall we start our tour?"

"Yes… yes, of course, Marlene. I am totally at your service. I hope I did not *really* embarrass you."

"You have a good singing voice but our first meeting is not the occasion to sing me a love song. Now I remember! That popular song was recorded in Germany by the group *Boney M*. I once read a library book telling me a Kenyan wrote about a young man extolling his woman as an angel but also informing her that he could not raise the bride price to marry her."

"I learn new things every day. I thought only Miriam Makebo sang *Malaika* and that it was South African."

"Different versions and different singers in Europe and America have recorded it. Harry Belafonte, for one, sings it."

"You take your music studies seriously. And, by the way, do you often visit your aunt?"

"I live with my aunt. My parents died in a car crash on the autobahn two years ago so she took me in."

"Oh, excuse me. I am so sorry. I should be more careful with my questions," he apologized thinking at the same time that if he obtained lodging with her aunt they would be living close up. Daiga was beginning to realize that this young woman was not the shy inexperienced schoolgirl he had briefly met at her aunt's house but a woman who knew something of even Africa and probably more than he of almost anything German and who had survived with apparent courage the loss of her parents. He changed the subject.

"We'll visit the university sports facilities first. Do you swim or play tennis? The university has an indoor pool and outdoor courts and there is badminton and a running track. We enter right here," he informed her as she followed him into the recreation building next door to the cafeteria where students were swimming laps and where, through tempered glass, they could see students rushing from side to side swiping black badminton balls.

"I swim regularly here and I occasionally play tennis," he put forward.

"I like to swim too," she volunteered.

"Now for the library' he said, boldly taking her hand and leading the way. As they walked Marlene could not believe the sensual feelings transmitted between them. "The library has music and art sections as you will see," he said.

Stares from three female students greeted them as they continued through the library. Daiga thought nothing of it since the students were strangers and he had always elicited stares on being seen with a German girl. It would only enhance his presence to have a young white female by his side. Marlene felt the thrill in her breast increase at his continued touch and she pressed firmer on his hand before releasing her hold in confusion at her boldness to examine some of the books.

"Next are the language laboratories. They lie in the basement of this tall building mainly assigned to student residences. My room is in Block D of the ninth storey. I have a marvelous view of Stuttgart that is well worth seeing. We could put the song *Malaika* on my record player and perhaps even dance a little and I can promise you I won't embarrass you by singing."

Marlene reminded him that she had come to the university to tour the facilities with him.

"The residences are an important part of university facilities."

"Since my home is nearby I don't suppose I will use them. Yet what you say is true. They are important. And, who knows, I may one day choose to reside at the university so seeing what they are like is a good idea."

Daiga breathed harder and his heart beat stronger as he led her to the elevator then exited on the ninth floor and walked hand in hand along the passage to his room. She again pressed hard on his hand. For a moment he thought with alarm that he had lost his key but after rummaging found it. He had ensured that his apartment was tidy. He had placed flowers on the table in hope of bringing her there. Drawing her over to the window he thought he would let the panoramic view begin to soothe her senses before turning to his turntable and letting soothing soft music fill the air.

"Isn't this enchanting?" he asked from behind with arms circling her waist and hands holding hers.

"Yes, yes, it is," she said hesitatingly.

"Shall we dance?"

Daiga released her lithe waist and took her right hand in his left hand. "Is it the music that enchants me or is it you?" he asked with a smile.

She came closer and looked up into his eyes. "I know what you are talking about."

He gently pushed his lower chest closer to her breasts and softly placed a kiss then a cheek against hers. She could feeling Daiga's racing heartbeat and realized her heart was beating faster too as they slowly circled the room to the music and lyrics of *Malaika*.

"You dance really well," she murmured in his ear.

Daiga gave her a soft wet kiss on the lips as she reciprocated his nearness with a hand round his neck and a further relaxation into his arms.

At that moment the record in the turntable ground to a halt and he had to push her adrift.

As they broke loose for a moment to reset the record player they both smiled and this time Marlene kissed Daiga on the cheek. Emboldened he planted kisses all over her face, cheeks, forehead and lips. Marlene excitedly grasped his waist and he felt her touch through his pants his erect penis. They had both discovered erogenous zones. Especially him!

"Oh, so sorry, I have a flashlight in my pocket," he jested making her smile as he pressed harder. Little did he know that from that point on there was more to come from this warm fraulein who spoke excellent English and whom he had thought straight and cold before he had taken her in his arms and incredibly was now helping him unbutton her purple twinset top and talk openly.

"You must have a close boyfriend from what I have experienced," he said not receiving any reply.

To his surprise she began to unbutton his shirt and, as he stood breathing deeply with eyes half closed, gently caressed his neck then his chest with slow, circular strokes and kisses.

"Are you undressing me?" she whispered to his further bewilderment since she was certainly leading him on in that department. He determined not to disappoint her by pressing a hand under the rim of her tight skirt then gently loosening her twin-suit top, taking it off and carefully placing it on a chair at the side of the bed.

Her breasts stood half out warm and inviting from within a pink slip. He gently kissed below her neck and above each breast as they hardened to his hands below.

"I will undress you on two conditions," Daiga replied in a sudden brainstorm that he thought might work. "The first is that we do not have sexual intercourse because you are too young and could get pregnant and the second is that you must undress me first. I don't plan to dominate this wonderful just discovered relationship but I aim to make the most of it now."

"I agree on both counts," she replied appreciating his straightforward talk and acting on it immediately. He wondered if she had done this before but dismissed the thought from his mind when within a minute his trouser belt was loosened. Unzipped by her he pulled his pants down and stepped out of them his erection clearly attempting to break through his underpants. Marlene looked down at what she had never seen before. It was new and exciting to seduce this handsome African man with all the passion and performance she had fantasized about in her bedroom after first briefly meeting him.

She lost no time in removing her clothes as the setting sun streamed through the bow window illuminating to his eyes her totally uncovered lovely breasts as she stood naked and at his urging twirling before him. She clung close as they danced a few more slow steps. Boldly she pulled his underpants down over his penis and let them flop on the floor. She led an astonished Daiga by hand to the bed before lying on her back and pulling him down on top of her and grasping with both hands his back. He gently slipped downward to kiss what he thought might be her clitoris. The sensation was so overwhelming that he quickly withdrew before he could say Jack penis!

She did not mind that at all as they lay clinging to each other in a hypnotic swoon of desire she for the first man she had ever touched in such a way and he for a woman he thought already in love with him. So they lay there for 20 minutes each caressing every part of the other. He watched her eyes close and her brow furrow as he told her he loved her. There was no spontaneous burst of passion just reciprocal caresses that indicated to him she wanted the moment to last forever.

After half an hour against all willpower he whispered: "It's time for you to go home beautiful woman." He boldly added that they would each remember the afternoon for the rest of their lives. "Make me happy by saying so."

His words mesmerized her and still under his influence she whispered back: "Yes, I *will* remember?"

"Marlena, you're my darling Marlena," he melodiously answered her.

"You really do sing like Harry Belafonte," she said. "The only wrong thing is that my name is Marlene not Marlena."

He confidently pushed her gentle rebuke aside grinning down at her nakedness before momentarily kissing her feet then rolling off the bed. "Come on beautiful innocent woman. I'm no African jungle beast ready to take you to my lair. Get your clothes on. If you stay longer you will regret it and your aunt will be up here looking for you and maybe for me too."

Taking hold of her left arm he pulled her up from the bed before crushing and kissing her once more. "Now you know about love in Africa."

Marlena summoned the first German words she had used that afternoon filling his senses with its clarity. "I know of you, *mein unschuldig liebhaber!*"

Chapter 8

YES AND NO

Daiga's language course was finally about to end. He had successfully written his exams and accepted a certificate that would qualify him to teach in Cameroonian secondary schools. Yet instead of joining his classmates from France and Spain to return home, he registered for a political science course at the university's Faculty of International Relations and was provisionally accepted. But it still meant he had to earn more money on his own to pay fees and keep himself from starving. The problem was how to earn enough within a month to see him through in the short term and in the long term enough to obtain a Bachelor of Arts degree. The three-year challenge was formidable.

He was occasionally seeing Marlene but he could not imagine her providing him with long term financial security. He saw only one way ahead. That was to get a better job and quickly trade off his good looks to capture a better-off German woman who would subsidize his needs. This he saw as a not impossible task since there were such women available. She would have to be as attracted to him as Marlene but come from a rich family. So, he stopped seeing Marlene to free himself for pecuniary conquest. He explained to her that her future enrollment in university would present opportunities for them and that he needed total time for his studies. His success with her and the ease in which she accepted his reason for breaking up first surprised and then in a way disappointed him. He wondered if she had sought to break with him too. But it also encouraged him to try harder for a woman suited to his mercantile needs.

He recalled the cultural attaché at the Cameroon embassy in Bonn telling him: "If down the street you find a German girl that you love, bring her here. We contract marriages. A good German girl will help you." Daiga realized other African students must have gone through what he was going through. What use was it to waste a possible opportunity with a more profitable partner than a young girl without means or a woman back home in Africa also without means? To come to Europe and do only nine months of language study was senseless. To go back and be a mere schoolteacher was wasting a lifetime's opportunity. Why not instead go back with a full-fledged degree to work in the Cameroon diplomatic service where German would be an asset, or even try for the legislature?

Targeting a suitable German girl for marriage would solve immigration problems that might soon arise. He now spoke almost fluent German. He could even sing German and Cameroonian love songs already tried out with Marlene and he believed that might now help too. Mungwi had gone from his mind except to treat her as out of his life. What use was any woman who could not help her man climb a rung of the ladder of success? He reasoned that he was not the cause of what he now figured was Mungwi's backwardness. Mungwi had to look for another man to restructure her life in Africa.

He would build his career helped by a woman of means. Mungwi could use her undoubted beauty to entice another man as he was using his handsome self to do the same thing. Success in life was for the taking and not what others made for one. It was stupid to depend on others. Even if he were to depend on a German girl helping him build his life he at least was drawing the foundation of success rather than sitting idly by like Mungwi no doubt waiting for manna from heaven. Those thoughts occasionally left him with a vague feeling of contradiction and failure in the pit of his stomach that he determined to overcome by willpower, hard work and the still potent experience of his vibrant conquest of Marlene in one afternoon.

With marriage in mind and Marlene also cast aside he started screening more seriously the female students within his reach to see which woman would best fit his need for long-term security. He thought confidently that he was well built for the job of luring women into his arms. He thanked God for his natural attributes.

He thought how his creator had formed his structure for Daiga but not for Daiga alone. Looking at his eyes, ears and nostrils in the mirror he asked himself what was there but pure symmetry. He thought himself as handsome as any man could be. In fact, it was true that Daiga was on the surface every fair lady's man. His size and height made him fit for almost every type of outfit or woman in the western fashion world. He had perfect teeth. His smile was charming. Very few girls turned down invitations to chat with him. But Daiga had that one unforgivable sin of potential infidelity. Soon he was going for any pretty woman who accepted him at any time. A woman was a woman. No use tying oneself to one woman. God did not create any particular woman for any particular man. No woman had the right to take all of a man to herself. That would be unjust.

He had discovered that older women outnumbered men in Germany. Since the war had killed of young German soldiers many of the older women were widows. Daiga figured that if one man could satisfy older women this would help to satisfy those who could not find a man because of the gender imbalance. The task would have been easy for him in that respect except that he sought not an old but a financially secure young woman. He could list no fewer than five female German students who had lunched with him each one not knowing exactly what relationship he had with any of the others.

He had even manipulated a doubles game of tennis against the attractive Teresa Hinkle, who had been on the opposite side of the net with her partner Hans. She was on his mind as a possible wife because of her well-off family background but as a suitor he lost any chance immediately he started to play. He was first to serve and unluckily had to smack his serves into the sun. He recalled the game going from love-all to love-40 as he served balls the athletic Hans and even Teresa killed with passing shots. "Bit out of condition with the serve, eh?" Hans had remarked after passing Daiga down the alley for the third time and they were changing sides. Daiga was not offended but he took Teresa off his list when he learned that she and Hans were more than just tennis partners but engaged to marry. He feared he would be brushed off by her or bumped off by her boyfriend if he tried to step between them.

Daiga's tennis partner, Anna, whom he had picked up from a list of players on the notice board, was no wife for him either mainly because she was no beauty and he learned probably had no money.

Then there was Monica Weber Wonker, a young woman of above medium height. She had stiff legs, broad shoulders, a stern yet beguiling look and was approachable. She appeared to Daiga to be generous with her money and ready to make friends with him. He soon got to know her family background. Her Jewish parents had settled in Bonn from East Germany shortly after the war and were still living there. Her mother's family had narrowly survived the Holocaust. Daiga learned from Monica that her father had a large number of shares in some pharmaceutical company she named as Bayer or something of that pronouncement.

He was encouraged to discover from Monica that her father believed it was a child's right to enjoy a father's riches when there was need and opportunity. He was astonished to also learn that her father furnished Monica with a car. Monica was even on occasion buying Daiga lunch when he deliberately left his wallet behind in his room because he was almost broke. He calculated that she had a hefty bank account for a student and could draw money from her bank at will as she twice did before his eyes. Daiga was beginning to believe Monica was one of the richest girls of her age on earth especially after she purchased expensive tickets for a musical show for the two of them. She was soon top of his short list.

Monica told him her father had recently advised her that though he could give her everything money could buy there were two things he could not give her. His quoted words were: "Those two things you must soon get by yourself. They are a complete education and a life partner."

Through conversations Daiga knew she had a determination to succeed in life and he detected that marriage might now he one of her pursuits after a childhood of sufficient adventure and discovery. She favored what was out of the ordinary. While her siblings preferred the sand beaches of the Caribbean for holidays she had alarmed her parents by visiting Australia and for a short time studying the lives of aboriginals. While her father drove the latest German Mercedes she had convinced him to buy her an Italian Fiat. This she did in a Stuttgart known as the cradle of the automobile and that meant the cradle of the Mercedes or Daimler and not the Fiat. In some ways it was an act of rebellion but to Daiga and probably her father it just showed she knew her own mind. She was not an admirer of expensive jewelry and dresses but encouraged Daiga to dress well by buying him a suede jacket. She loved the company of foreign students and that perturbed him. She went down town with Daiga and purchased a watch for his birthday. She had developed a singular interest in him but she knew she had competition from other girls.

Close to Christmas Monica decided to call on Daiga for a serious discussion of their future relationship. She had inklings that Daiga was looking for a wife who could support him and she determined to confirm her suspicion.

"I shall be going to Bonn for the Christmas break to celebrate with my parents," she revealed to his surprise. "There is one thing I would like to know from you. We have been seeing each other for close to two months off and on and have come to enjoy each other's company. I would love to invite you to my home for the holidays, but I don't exactly know what you think about me and I know without jealousy other girls enjoy your occasional company."

This embarrassed Daiga somewhat. He had been bent on keeping all his girlfriends interested in him so he might make the best choice. However, Monica's approach had come at the right time for he was near penniless except for the small sum he received for serving at the university bar. He knew that once you declared to one German woman that you were in for her you had to stand by it. If you tried to play games with other women after putting your eggs in one basket then you were looking for real trouble. To him African girls were much easier to manipulate. But Monica was not African. She was not beautiful but pleasant looking, well built and seemed soft-spoken in well-chosen words. She was always ready to assist him when he needed her for a meal. In fact, Daiga had thought of proposing to her at the right time. Yet though the opportunity was there he was lost in figuring out an answer to the question of visiting her parents. Both yes and no were difficult. The alternatives meant the beginning of a real relationship or the end. To accept her invitation would mean going all the way and keeping other girls on his list from his front door. To refuse would mean he had rejected her and that she would probably never give him such an opportunity again. He could strike while the iron was hot by impressing her parents yet at the same time not appear to be easy game.

"I don't know. Maybe you should first tell me what you think of me and what your parents would think of a black man," said Daiga trying to play sensitive yet hard to get.

"I opened the topic with my question first. You must answer now or we drop it and split. I assure you the colour of your skin is of no consequence to me and what my parents think is their problem," Monica insisted.

Choosing his words with care Daiga answered: "Well... I know you as a nice friend. I think we can build a relationship. I believe I would come to love you with all my heart."

"Are you sure?" Monica asked looking straight into Daiga's eyes her heart melting. While she warmed up a chill ran down his spine. He shifted his eyes from her face realizing it was now or never to affirm his growing love of her.

"I ask you to be sure because I hear African men don't know what love is. They throw words at women they want to cheat," she said.

"I am serious," Daiga countered, prompted by thoughts of his depleted finances and quickly realizing he had her within his grasp.

"Do you know what love means to us here in Germany and can you tell me if it is different in Cameroon?"

"If you tell me more of love here in Germany it would add to what I know of love in Cameroon."

"What love in Cameroon do you speak of? Have you a woman there?"

"I had until I met you."

"Listen carefully," she said shifting her chair toward Daiga's chair and taking her opportunity to explain what to her was important: "What we mean by love here in Germany is one love, one woman, until death, or, if occasion warrants it, divorce. Love grows stronger and moves step by step. It stems from friendship, it moves to engagement and then to marriage. I hear in Africa that a man is a sometimes boyfriend to one woman, fiancé to another and husband to a third. I do not know the truth of it but here such conduct adds up to betrayal. Here love means one man and one woman together forever and ever."

The word forever threw another chill down Daiga's spine. This was not exactly what he was prepared for yet he knew it suited his purpose and that accepting it would secure his future. There was still Mungwi back in Africa to think about and other German girls that he had short-listed and might not be happy to renounce *forever* to suit Monica. While he was contemplating what strategy to play she wakened his senses with another tough question.

"Do you promise then to become my husband forsaking all other women in Germany and Africa?"

Daiga's mind was in such turmoil at her blunt challenge that tactfully he could not immediately answer affirmatively or negatively. It was like the chess game he had learned in the student common room. He had to checkmate her with the right words to snare her! He was not the king, but merely a pawn with ambition to be king.

"Answer yes or no," she demanded giving him the affirmative chance he sought. "I have put my cards on the table. Do I take your silence to be no?"

"No, I mean, yes. Yes, yes, yes forsaking all other women in the world to marry you my adorable Monica."

"Then I will take you as my man and give you my love. What do you do next?"

"'Marry you as I surely will!"

"No! First you propose marriage from down on your knees. Then you buy me an engagement ring that I will pay for. Do you know what an engagement ceremony is?"

"I know what you man but to me it is unnecessary. When we feel we can live together we should just go ahead and live like husband and wife."

"Wrong! Do you hear me? That may be the African way but it is not the German or Jewish way. When you go through all the engagement steps you commit yourself to your partner and to your conscience forever in marriage as the rabbi will tell you. And that is more than just living together. First, I shall take you home and introduce you to my parents as my fiancé. They may not be happy to envisage an African as their son-in-law but, unlike in some parts of Africa as I understand it, German parents do not decide the marriage partner of their children or have a bride price. I have the final decision on whom to marry. Whatever their reaction you will have my support and we will stick together until death do us part." With this said she stood up and bending down took hold of Daiga's left hand.

"Stand up!" she ordered him turning the tables on him. Daiga did not know what Monica was up to but he did as he was told. "Come closer and kiss me on the lips. Feel free. I am yours and you are mine." Daiga lost his usual reflexes on hearing her dogmatic summary. In Cameroon he had been accustomed to being in command of any women he was with as it had been so with Marlene in Germany. This was a new type of woman whose money he had enjoyed and kisses confined to the cheeks. He had never kissed her lips since they first met. He did not really know her as well as he had known Mungwi back in Cameroon, at least not beyond the casual visits, lunches and dinners together and their shopping trips. He still did not know what was expected of him at that point in time except… a kiss.

Instead of Daiga kissing her Monica embraced him against her breast, sucked his lips and pushed him gently onto the bed beside the wall away from the study desk as he had once been pulled by Marlene. He was once more being seduced and soon enjoying it. When she started unbuttoning his shirt and pants Daiga did not know whether to let her do so or stop her. He lost the power of action as she caressed him. Wrapped in her arms he surrendered himself to her to do whatever she liked of him.

"We are now engaged," she said as she kissed him over and over on the chest. "I love your beautiful black skin," she whispered.

"The door is unlocked," he managed to say all the while astonished at the sexual persuasion and power this aroused German woman had over him. He had to explain his meaning to her.

"I will lock it," Monica said moving towards the door while pulling off her blouse and slacks. Daiga lay there like a sacrificial lamb hardly given the chance to decide on anything. It was after midnight when her entrapment of him lessened sufficiently to permit sleep. He had been seduced but to his surprise he felt satisfied at their climax. At 7 a.m., when he was still dreaming, Monica tapped him on the bottom.

"I am going down to the travel agency to book the flights and pick up the air tickets and an engagement ring. Here are enough Deutschmarks. Go down town and buy two new suits and a nice shirt for yourself. I'll be back shortly. You should dress and be ready for my return in about 90 minutes. We will take the 2 p.m. flight to Bonn. Okay?"

"You don't have to buy me suits and shirts."

"Oh yes I do to visit my parents!" And off she went leaving a confused Daiga feeling blinded by this sudden unknown force that he felt was akin to television's *Bionic Woman*.

"What am I doing?" he asked himself. "Should I tell Mungwi that I have dumped her for a German woman? Mungwi is far away but she has a right to know. What will her parents and my parents think when they find out I am married to a white woman? Will the law of placement put everything in its rightful place?" With difficulty he banished Mungwi from his mind and switched his thoughts to Monica and his ambition of a political science degree and the financial security she could bring him if her father as generously shared his riches with him as he did with his daughter. And was Monica not only rich but as he had found out sexy too!

In two hours Monica returned from the travel agency to see Daiga trying on newly bought suits. The first one fitted him like the lid of a pressure oven. So did the second suit. She planted a kiss on his cheek while he was pantless between suits. Daiga moved back nervously though still holding her hands. He was somewhat bored with her numerous kisses. He usually was the one who decided when to kiss but not with Monica.

"You're so handsome, my dear Daiga," she said, stroking his cheeks with both her hands. Now get fully dressed and we will go down to the restaurant for a late breakfast or early lunch and after that prepare ourselves for meeting my parents in Bonn. Go on!"

Monica placed him right in front of other girls in the elevator and planted another kiss on his cheek to surprise them. The restaurant was a five-minute walk across the campus. As they walked, Monica seized Daiga's right hand, put it over her shoulders and grasped Daiga's waist with her left hand. Midway across they met Teresa and Anna. She knew Daiga had flirted for a short time with the latter. The students appraised the couple in surprise Anna still feeling jilted by him. They must have wondered when this close union had started.

Daiga would normally have stood and chatted with Anna as he usually did with friends but Monica's grip was tight and she gave him no chance to stop. He was upset at silently passing them but could not do a thing about it.

In the restaurant Monica compelled him to pay attention to her alone. He would normally have been free to turn his eyes at will on any girl who came in and perhaps sat down next to him. He wondered how much longer he was going to be under her spell and almost gasped at what had been her use of the word forever. Clearly Monica had claimed a lifetime for them together. Could he withstand it? Once again he thought of the gentle and docile Mungwi back home. His heart flushed as if he had contracted a fever. Monica gave him no respite in the next half hour back in his room. He proposed marriage from down on his knees before she sealed the bond with another hug and a demand he place the engagement ring on her finger.

"I accept you with all my heart," said she in total bliss.

Soon they had taxied off to the airport to board Lufthansa flight 312 bound for Bonn for him to meet her parents.

On learning of their engagement Monica's father asked a host of questions about Daiga and given satisfactory replies by Monica and him peremptorily advised them to go straight to the synagogue the next day and book a date for an official Jewish marriage. Daiga said he preferred a simple unrushed ceremony at the Cameroon embassy in Bonn.

"Oh, no, you can't marry my daughter there," Monica's mother, Vera, admonished Daiga. "You have to marry her properly. From today you are no more a Cameroonian, right? By marriage to my daughter you will become a Germaroon rather than a Cameroon!" She laughed at her own joke before adding: "Monica is German and all the children the two of you bring forth shall be Germans. Do you understand? Your dogs, your cats will be German too. No damn Cameroons any longer. Okay? Cameroon has to be cleaned out of your blood stream for Cameroon can't do anything better for you than Germany can do ten times more."

That was more than enough for Daiga to stand and he thought about walking out of the house there and then since he had an air ticket purchased by Monica in his pocket but there was still more hyperbole in store for him as Vera ranted on:

"Daiga, you must not only be more German," she insisted, "you must be Jewish-German. We are Jews and our ancestors were Jews. Within my family you become one of the Diaspora Jews here in Germany. You will be a descendant by marriage of the Jewish victims who lived in exile and were scattered after their Babylonian dispersion outside Palestine. The poetic name for the Holy Land is Zion. Zionism is focused on the Jewish return to Zion. It is an example of Jewish national state interests and social gospel. On May 14, 1948, the State of Israel was proclaimed to the world. Zionists have now reconstituted a large part of Palestine as a Jewish national home. Are you familiar with the violence, terror and bombings that have victimized Israel and the Holy Land of Palestine since then?"

Daiga sat transfixed in distaste. He shook his head in answer to her question. He was saved from replying and from more verbal indoctrination when Monica intervened.

"Mother! How *can* you? Daiga is a Cameroonian from Africa and that comes first with him and with me. Your study of Jewish history and your ancestry has resulted in your going on about it all the time. We have a pending wedding to celebrate and not the history of Israel or the German cultural failings of my future husband. Tell her it is so, father!"

"I cannot instruct your mother," Mr. Wonker told his daughter. "You know I have tried," he added, with a searching look at his wife that quieted her down. "We both accept Daiga as he is. I apologize to you Daiga for any distress my wife may have caused you. She will apologize later. Won't you Vera?"

"Indeed! I will apologise if I caused offence."

Daiga kept his silence inwardly aware that Monica and her father had taken his side on this occasion. At the same time he detected the first hint that Monica and her mother were what one might say like mother like daughter in their dogmatic, if divergent, views and character. Neither then, nor in the day ahead, had he any chance to change his mind about marrying Monica. It was a *fait accompli* accepted as the only way to becoming legally settled in Germany and to meet the financial requirements of studying for a degree. He considered himself lucky he did not have a baptismal middle name such as Peter, John or Francis else the name Daiga might have been wiped off the face of the map by Monica's mother and replaced with a European name, say Francis, Peter, David or John. Also lucky for him Monica did prefer his African name to any European name.

"Well, Daiga, let us go out for a beer and celebrate this good news," Monica's father broke into his silent thoughts putting an arm around his shoulders to emphasize his invitation. "We can leave those two to make up."

Daiga soon found it was for more than a beer his future father-in-law had in mind. "My wife is an orthodox Jew," he said when they had settled in a corner pub. "She suffered a trauma when relatives of hers were murdered by Palestinians. She takes it all too seriously after 10 years. You will have to forgive her outburst since she meant for the best. You will find Monica and me more secular though nevertheless Jewish. In fact Monica is a trifle cool on religion of any kind although I understand she goes to the synagogue."

"I don't take offence easily," Daiga replied. "So we can both relax."

"Good for you, because tonight is the occasion of a traditional *shabbos* dinner. It will help if Monica and you come with us to celebrate your upcoming wedding. You will enjoy a beautiful evening with strangers who fast become friends at this traditional Friday evening service and meal."

"Of course we will go out to dinner with you."

"Don't be surprised if Vera introduces you to our rabbi. He is a kind, elderly gentleman who will welcome you with open arms when he hears the news from Monica and you. By the way, do you know that Jews have a strong affinity with the African National Congress in South Africa and indeed with Nelson Mandela?"

Daiga looked up into Mr. Wonker's eyes gently shaking his head.

Encouraged, Mr. Wonker went on: "Many of the civil rights lawyers who represent the ANC in those trials that are taking place in South Africa are Jews. One female Jewish MP, who recently spoke out publically against Vorster's apartheid policies, is a close personal friend of Mandela."

"I know little of the trials going on in South Africa. What you say really interests me. Let me buy this round then you can tell me more."

"Well, I detest apartheid. Genes, not skin colour, is the important thing. I have Russian-Jewish genes no less and there is nothing black or white about them."

Daiga, thinking Mr. Wonker was talking about the pants he wore, responded: "Well, the jeans I often wear are a fairly subdued grey."

Mr. Wonker was confused but, giving Daiga the benefit of a joke, laughed out loud and continued to talk through it. "Did Monica tell you she spent some time in a kibbutz in Israel? I visited her there. It was most interesting. The kibbutzim council did not approve of her liberal ways. In this instance the power of the community took precedence over self-identity. You would have worse problems than Monica if you lived in a kibbutz. Yet you could visit Israel with me for the experience. There are black Jews in Ethiopia and some in Israel. For now let us drink again to your forthcoming marriage to my daughter and perhaps to your future visit to Israel."

Chapter 9

JEWISH WEDDING

Tuesday was the chosen day for the wedding and Daiga had little choice in the matter except to say with Monica's support that he did not want an elaborate affair. Tuesday was chosen because, he was told, the Torah would support it on that day. Then there was the quick wedding search for cakes, invited guests, hairstyles, wedding music and songs, centerpieces, bouquets, rings, photographers. He had only one search mission and that was to find a best man for the ceremony which he accomplished at the student union office although he hardly knew the volunteer.

He knew Monica's father was paying for the wedding and he had the sense to thank him saying that as an immigrant he was not rich. Early wedding gifts were stacked in a corner of the living room. Daiga had no idea where they had all come from or indeed what was really going on.

Conversion to Judaism had been impressed on him by Rabbi Franz as an act of enormous courage, sincerity and spiritual commitment. Judaism welcomed with open arms those who were genuine in their pursuit.

He learned that Jewish converts should know that Judaism required the specific belief in One God as defined in Jewish Scripture and traditional authorized rabbinic sources. He would be compelled to accept Judaism to the exclusion of other faiths and religious practices and he would pledge to establish a Jewish home and participate actively in the Jewish community. Should Monica and he be blessed with children, they would raise them as Jews.

"It won't happen overnight," he was glad to hear the rabbi say.

He accepted the approach by listening, saying little and wondering if he had gone over his head in what was going on all around him.

Daiga also wondered how Monica was reacting to this religious zeal. He determined he would make no promises but merely say he would endeavor to do all he was asked and be content to tell Monica so when they were back in Stuttgart for their honeymoon.

The marriage ceremony was conducted under a wedding canopy and Monica, wearing a white off-shoulder dress under a string of pearls, and he, in a dark suit, recited sacred vows to each other to spiritualize their relationship. Plain gold wedding bands gifted by her father were exchanged to symbolize their commitment.

When the rabbi wrapped Daiga and Monica in a shawl he responded by immediately kissing her and listening to a word of unneeded advice from her father and mother direct to him that marriage lasts longer than the wedding day.

Daiga had been instructed on the breaking-of-the-glass ceremony that would end the ceremony so he knew to step forward and stomp the cloth napkin that wrapped the glass content. To his bewilderment shouts of *Mazel Tovi* filled the synagogue. He knew it meant it was his last chance to put his foot down.

If Daiga believed without saying so that the marriage rituals were a bore he had more coming his way at the reception. Wine, beer and munchies were on the tables as guests chatted in groups and a photographer roamed around. In the background a harpist stroked her instrument soothingly. The rabbi contentedly joined in the merrymaking. Fish and chicken were served for dinner and Monica and he cut a chocolate cake rising high in rings as cameras flashed.

Daiga had been introduced to guests who mainly had shaken his hand then walked off to be with their friends. He wondered if he was becoming the only black Jew in the world. He decided to be honest by revealing his thought and it led some guests to smile and others exclaim it was not so. "Well," he said, "if it is not so, where are the other black Jews?" The rhetorical question caught everyone by surprise. Monica saved the day. "You are *my* black Jew," she said throwing a kiss at him as spoons tinkled cups and a round of applause erupted. "You are indeed my one and only black Jew."

"Your father told me there are black Jews in Ethiopia and Israel."

Monica lightened the moment by turning her back on the crowd and throwing her bouquet in the air. An athletic young woman jumped and caught it then turned on Daiga and to his surprise kissed his right cheek.

Contemporary music broke out and Daiga was pulled on the floor into a first dance with Monica then joined by others holding hands in a circle with them in the middle. At its conclusion he was hoisted on a chair and blindfolded. He had to guess by feeling faces which woman was touching him. He was glad when it turned out to be Monica.

Loud traditional Hebrew music heralding the Hora dance reflected wishes of good luck. The different dances left Daiga bewildered as the night flew by. He breathed a sigh of relief when Monica and he were ushered off for their honeymoon in a Fiat decorated with ribbons and graffiti. They had secretly chosen as their destination their rented home in Stuttgart.

Chapter 10

THE BERLIN WALL

Two weeks after the wedding Monica's father handed them the keys of new Mercedes Benz saloon car saying their wedding car had convinced him they required a better car. Even though Monica preferred her smaller Italian car she accepted the wedding gift to please not just her father but also Daiga.

"I hope this will help you get on with your lives together," Mr. Wonker said, twice wishing them a long and happy marriage.

"Father, you know that Daiga is studying political science and I intend to take a degree when he gets his degree. You know that we did not go far for a honeymoon. So we saved money. What would make us really happy would be to travel to East Berlin to see my Uncle Peter and Aunt Marga? Travel through East Germany to Berlin has been made easier. In fact, hundreds of West Germans, with students among them, are now crossing into East Germany and some onward to East Berlin to see families and friends. A trip, even if only for two days, would be wonderful for our studies and how exciting it would be for me to meet my uncle and aunt and them to meet my husband."

"You say students can obtain permits to visit East Berlin? That is news to me."

"Some are doing so."

"You mean to drive there?"

"Yes. By way of Frankfurt then Kassel, where we can switch from car to train, leaving the car for our return."

"What do you think, Daiga? Do you favour a visit to East Berlin," Mr. Wonker enquired, secretly hoping Daiga might decline because such a trip might endanger Monica as was his view.

"A visit to East Berlin would certainly help my studies and future career," Daiga disappointed him by saying. "I have never seen the Communists at work. My problem in Europe still is that I am black. It was not easy just traveling through Paris when I first came here. Will the East Germans play racist games with the likes of me, I wonder?"

"Well, the answer seems to be that they probably will not," Mr. Wonker had to admit. "They have financed and set up an embassy in Zanzibar and they are building apartments there. Apparently they seek to impress newly independent African states. Their Soviet masters would probably be embarrassed if the East Germans discriminated against a black student arriving with his German wife to meet their relatives. It would be bad for their international image. No, you are probably safer than most in visiting East Berlin. But is my Jewish daughter safe?"

"I will look after her," Daiga shot back. "I doubt they will even know she is Jewish."

Time was getting short and with that said Mr. Wonker drove them to the waiting hall of the Bonn airport still considering Monica's request. Before they boarded their plane back to Stuttgart Mr. Wonker crossed the Rubicon not to mention the Berlin Wall. He told Monica: "Go, by all means to East Berlin. Take some fresh coffee for your Uncle Peter and butter and eggs for Aunt Marga. I believe they are in short supply there. Remember though to answer honestly that you are Jewish as well as German if they ask. Be forthright and careful at all times."

Chapter 11

HIGH NOON ON FRIEDRICHSTRASSE

In Stuttgart, Daiga and Monica soon furnished their apartment on the Kernestrasse. Mr. Wonker paid the cost and the rent for a year.

They had spending money, too, from Monica's father who set up a joint bank account for them and preparations were significantly underway for their trip via Frankfurt, through East Germany by train from Kassel and under or over the Wall to East Berlin. They had obtained permits from the East German Embassy newly set up in Bonn following East-West treaties signed by West German President Willy Brandt and they would be leaving in one week for a stay of two days in Berlin.

They decided to share the driving northward to Frankfurt, spend a night in a hotel before journeying on to Kassel, safely park their car, and then take the train through East Germany to Berlin.

Daiga's mind was a maelstrom of wonder and fear originating from what he had heard of East Berlin from a western standpoint. He had not studied the politics of East Berlin at university but he was fascinated by what he had been told and read informally and welcomed the chance to see what was going on firsthand from the other side. Surely it would help any later career in West Germany or as a diplomat in Cameroon which was always at the back of his mind.

The couple arrived safely at the crossing point of Friedrichstrass station, near Potsdam. They were soon lined up in a queue inside a glass-and-steel bunker built to process visitors in and out. The supposed infamously ill-mannered and brusque East German border officials checked their passports and luggage politely and ensured neither was abusing currency regulations. After a few questions about their political science studies had ensured them by their answers that the security of the worker and peasant state would not be undermined in any major way, a guard pressed a button that allowed them through.

The door took them into a drub eastern part of the station with a dearth of commercialism and advertising that did not surprise them. The cheap food they took advantage of along with cups of terrible coffee and a book store where Monica bought an inexpensive copy of a Marxist classic and where taxis waited.

"It's all so easy," Daiga murmured to Monica as they sat nervously behind their cab driver in his *Lada* on way to the home of their relatives in the inner-city East Berlin district of Mitte. On arrival the driver spoke hardly a word and the fare Monica paid was not expensive.

Monica's Uncle Peter and Aunt Marga were overjoyed to welcome them to their modest home but to Daiga's dismay they spoke a German tongue he could hardly understand. Monica formally introduced her husband to them and they both cast long scrutinizing eyes on this black persona.

After confirming they would stay overnight their hosts showed Monica and Daiga to a spare room with a double bed and a bathroom to themselves and said they had invited two young friends of theirs for supper with them that night. When Monica and Daiga had freshened up and come downstairs they saw outside the dining room a great table laid in the open with all the food East Berlin people had complained they could never get, but which had miraculously materialized on this special occasion.

"Ah, but this will be much better coffee," Uncle Peter told Monica after she had presented them with her gifts and his wife had brewed up.

When cordially introduced to Erich and Angela there came a few hesitant words in English from Erich when he found that Daiga spoke English better than German.

"This normalization of travel from west to east is only partial," he told them warming up in conversation. "I should not say so, but the east still treats the west as the enemy and probably vice versa."

"But we crossed so easily," Daiga responded. "Sure, heads were raised when I said I was a political science student, but nothing else happened. It was easier here than my transit in France."

"Well, westerners call Friedrichstrasse station bunker the Palace of Tears. They have probably noted carefully that you are studying politics and may now be looking into your African background."

"Trädnenpalast," responded Uncle Peter twirling sauerkraut between fork and spoon then clearly enjoying a mouthful while listening intently.

"Things are not so bad here really," Aunt Marga broke in. "After all, a lot here is free, for instance, places in kindergarten, and a lot is cheap, for example good bread. Everything in the West is not perfect. I read that unemployment is high. Is that true Monica? East Germany has even helped African economies. East Germany gave financial aid to independent Zanzibar and now is building needed apartment estates."

"Monica's father pointed that out to us too," Daiga said.

This prompted Monica to reflect: "My father never talks politics these days. He is too busy making money from his pharmaceutical investments. My mother on the other hand talks too much politics."

"Your mother tragically was bereaved in the conflict between Israel and Palestine so that is the reason," Marga said.

"What are you talking about," her husband intervened. "There is no such country as Palestine."

"I know you believe that," said Marga. "Well, tell it to the Palestinians!"

Daiga was astonished to realize there was conflict between the two over the Middle East battleground.

Uncle Peter simply frowned and went on eating.

"Is it possible to see the Berlin wall?" Daiga asked anxiously seeking to change the subject. "Back in West Germany I can hardly talk of my visit to East Berlin and admit I never saw the wall that one of my professors calls The Wall of Shame that runs through the centre of Berlin and which, he says, turns East Berlin into a prison for people like you. Monica and I saw some elegant streets from our taxi that did not bear out the shabby image given East Berlin by the West."

"Ah, but that is the relatively sunny exterior of Honaker's East Germany. Once tourists get away from those showcase streets, if they ever do, they find decaying, shabby buildings and, frankly, exploitation of human misery behind the GDR façade. In churches, prayer meetings are politicizing, women are joining politicized feminine groups and an anti-nuclear movement is growing right under the noses of the Stazi secret police. I tell you the German moment will come!"

Daiga was astonished by Erich's fiery words. "Is this talk not dangerous here?" he asked. "What do you mean by the German moment?"

"When the Wall is torn down."

His words silenced all of them around the table until the silence was broken when Uncle Peter suggested: "It is a pleasant evening. I think our visitors would enjoy a walk but, I regret, not near the Wall."

"They should not walk with me," Erich said. "I know the Stazi are watching me. You four go for a stroll. We will await your return while enjoying this excellent coffee."

Monica and Daiga and her uncle and aunt donned coats and were strolling down the street enjoying the fresh air when a police vehicle drew up beside them. "Are you Herr Daiga who arrived today?" asked one of the officials. "We wish to take you to headquarters to answer some questions."

"Yes, I am Daiga. But what do you wish to know that I can't answer here and now?"

"It is only for a short interrogation to clear up an unimportant matter. It is nothing serious. Jump in our vehicle. We will not detain you long and you will be returned here to your hosts."

"Better do as they say," Peter instructed a frozen-on-the-spot Daiga.

"Okay," he replied clamouring into the back of the car and trying to figure out what was about to happen to him as it took off rumbling over cobbled street to where he felt not he but maybe only God knew where.

The destination was in a place once known as the forbidden area. Catching the ordinary tram that started at the Alexanderplatz and trundled eastwards five or so kilometres along the broad boulevard of the Leninallee, the casual traveler could get out at the Gensler Strasse stop. Only when one tried to enter the small maze of streets north of the Leninallee did orientation difficulties begin.

This busy outer district of East Berlin had Daiga perplexed. He had no idea where he was but had the police car turned into Frienwalder Strasse they would have met a stop sign, a checkpoint manned by armed guards in the uniform of the East German Ministry of State Security, and a set of high paneled barriers blocking further progress. This was the main entrance to the forbidden area near the Berlin Wall.

Daiga felt the car cross a flagstoned road and he observed a building in front as it passed through a gate that clanged shut when the car stopped. He was marched towards a door and into an office. The interrogation room was brightly lit even dazzling out of the corners. An interrogator's chair and desk were in front of a stool.

"Now," said a steely looking officer who had entered the room and sat down comfortably at the desk, "how did you come to be with Erich Reuter?"

Daiga paused before replying wondering how the interrogator knew of Erich and him being together. "My wife and I were having supper with him at the invitation of my wife's East Berlin aunt and uncle whom we are visiting. I believe Erich was there as companions because he and his wife are about the same age as my wife and I."

"What did you talk about?"

"Odds and ends!"

"You must answer my question. What did you talk about?"

"This and that!"

The interrogator thumped the desk with his fist. "You are being uncooperative. Let us begin again. What did you talk about? Start with this then go on to that."

"Pardon me. Í am trying to remember the conversation. Ah, yes. It was mainly about the World Football Cup and the chances of East Germany beating Cameroon."

"Your country is Cameroon?"

"Yes, in West Africa. I am studying political science at university in Stuttgart helped by my German wife Monica. I hope to be a diplomat one day in Cameroon. I believe you are a diplomat here in East Berlin. I thought a visit to East Berlin would be educational and help my future career."

"Cameroon is it? Do you know that the German Democratic Republic gives financial aid to Africa?"

"Ah, yes. Now I remember. We spoke about the republic's aid to Zanzibar, the cloves and coconut island off the East African coast. Erich's wife mentioned that your country has built apartments in Zanzibar and is helping with financial aid to the Zanzibar government. I am very interested in this. My country of Cameroon could use East German help in fairly sharing our resources among the people."

"Zanzibar was also an Arab slave island some years back. What else did you discuss?"

"We spoke about free kindergarten education in East Berlin and the bargain price of bread. Cameroon could use kindergartens and low cost bread."

"Yes? I am sure of that. What else?"

"We spoke about a chance football game between West Germany and England in the World Cup similar to the clash in England in the 1966 final when England won the cup."

"You are now playing football with me and winning," the interrogator grimaced with a humph and half laugh. His face broke out in a smile when to Daiga's delight he remarked: "At this moment I can see Cameroon beating the Democratic Republic of Germany."

Daiga saw an opening: "I can't. To tell you the truth that was about all we discussed because I had difficulty understanding the host East German dialect. Apart from the fact that I told them a few things about life in Cameroon, half of which they did not understand because I spoke mostly in English and could not follow their German, we discussed very little of consequence."

"You have the makings of a diplomat," the officer said soberly before waving across the room to the two functionaries who had brought Daiga in. "Take this man back to where you picked him up and apologize to him for his inconvenience. He is an innocent visitor from Africa come by way of West Germany with a permit to learn about our socialist way of life. He is not a spy to be arrested and brought here for interrogation. He is, like independent Africa, our friend, not our enemy."

Daiga rose and offered a handshake to his interrogator who was at that moment clearly friendly when handing him an East German pin for his lapel.

"Na gode. Sai an jima," he said in a native tongue that left the interrogator and East German guards reeling and the officer saying: "Go back to Stuttgart and tell the West Germans you were well treated in East Berlin."

Chapter 12

HOUSE OR HOME

When their first child was born Daiga thought he would name him after his uncle back home in Ba Binyalla, an uncle who had been kind to him, but Monica warned: "You heard my mother say this is not a Cameroon child. She says we must name the boy after German Minister of Defence Burner Schneider. Burner will be his name."

Daiga searched in vain for an argument. "You're going to name my child after a German defence minister. What sort of a name is Burner anyway?"

"It is my mother's idea."

"Who else could think of such a name?

"You do not like my mother, do you?"

"Not from the very first moment when she called me a Germaroon."

"She says the boy will soon have to be circumcised."

"Your rabbi told me nothing about that. Is that your mother's decree"

"My mother insists on it. It will have to be done."

Daiga had begun to realize that he had almost everything he needed in life except being master in his own home and father of his child. Their home was modern with laundry machines, television set, music and book library, fridge and freezer and what have you at Monica's father's expense. Daiga had risen from rags to riches through marriage. The Mercedes Benz wedding present, with fuel tickets often paid from Bonn, were largely at Monica's disposal. She openly wondered why her father had given them a car when she already had her Fiat. Yet to say Daiga was a happily married man was far from the truth. He remembered the wise saying that money can get you a nice house but not a nice home. Daiga could not easily take the car to drive anywhere he wanted because at first he did not have a license to drive in Germany. When eventually he passed his driving test at the second attempt he found that his duty was to drop Monica off where she wanted to go before going anywhere himself. Monica discouraged Daiga from private outings. He drove almost only for Monica's needs or pleasure. She enjoyed her husband's company though. But Daiga saw himself as Monica's chauffeur. She was meticulous in keeping the apartment clean. At least he could appreciate that.

"I know you have few friends but warn those you know not to come trampling on the carpet with their shoes on and sit on the sofas with their wet coats," she told him as though she had read his thoughts. "If you have African friends, okay, we can have them as long as they don't mess up our house."

"I don't know who you are referring to and none are from Africa," Daiga responded. "You, Monica, must not receive any visitors whom I don't know."

"Of course I won't. But, as you know, I like making friends as long as they are decent. That was why I started going out with you before we married."

"You and your parents sometimes forget that I am the man of the family and head of household. It is not for you or them to instill discipline in this house and it is decidedly not for your mother to say what our son's name will be."

"There is no head of household here. If there were to be one, that person would be me, Monica Wonker. The boy's name is Burner full stop."

"A correction is required to your erroneous wrong correction. Your name is Monica Daiga. There is no Monica Wonker in this house! I can't stand the name Burner. Is he ready to burn down the house?"

"Okay, I am Monica Daiga. Thank you for the correction but not for that English interpretation of the boy's name. Now I am hungry. Go to the kitchen and heat up dinner for the two of us. The lasagna is in the fridge so there is not much to do. I will reflect on what you have been telling me. Some of it is sensible but I thought you too intelligent to associate the name Burner with fire."

"I am not preparing dinner." Daiga retorted in frustration at her turn of the tables on him. "If you are hungry prepare dinner for yourself or for the two of us."

"It is your turn in the kitchen. I cooked yesterday."

"It is a wife's duty to make meals for her husband. If I am your husband, I don't have to cook while you sit there doing virtually nothing only because you cooked yesterday. It is your duty to cook year round until death us do part as you used to say."

"What did you just say?" Monica asked referring to Daiga's use of the word *if.*

"You heard me!"

"Talking about names another question for you to answer is why when last we slept together you two times whispered the name Marlena and you hummed that Maliaka tune?"

"You have a long memory."

"Well, now I am asking you who this Marlena is."

"More like dreaming up a question!" retorted Daiga taking a step back before heading flummoxed for his study and leaving Monica wringing her hands in frustration.

The exchange was typical of the crisis Daiga and Monica were in at the beginning of the third year of their marriage. Daiga realized that it did not take a wise man to tell him they had reached a point of no return. But, for the sake of obtaining his Bachelor of Arts degree, he decided he would hold on to what he had at least until the end of the year. What he would do then was the question. He had stopped writing to Mungwi and to everyone else in Cameroon. He felt adrift in a white German-Jewish world that each day became more divorced from his inner nature. He had begun to yearn for his lost princess and the simpler life he had left behind in Africa.

Monica, on the other hand, wished to put Daiga back in his place as her husband and lover. She had loved him at the start but she had the same doubts as he about the future of their marriage.

Chapter 13

SUITORS SPURNED

Back in Cameroon something that Daiga knew nothing about was happening. Mungwi's father, Ba Tita, went to Ba Daiga and told him: "It is four years since your people visited me with the wine to introduce yourselves as future in-laws. Hardly anything has been seen of you again, which traditionally is not normal. We Africans raise a female child to one day eat oil on her. You see now that Mungwi is almost growing out of marriage age just because she is waiting for your son who is lost somewhere in the white man's country or for three years and not showing any signs of coming back. I thought I should come and invite you to come here and we could refund everything you people brought for the knock-door ceremony so that we can accept some other suitor for my daughter before she finally grows out of marriage age."

Ba Daiga was at a loss to answer Ba Tita. He, too, was puzzled about what had happened to his son in Germany. Daiga had not written for almost three years despite his letter asking him to write a word to Mungwi. What could he tell Ba Tita? That he should go ahead and give Mungwi out to another suitor? What then would happen if Daiga came back home looking for Mungwi?

"My brother," he told Ba Tita, "you are no more worried than I am about our son in the white man's land. You may think I know something about him, but I must say I am as ignorant as you about his fate over there It is not the first time that something like has happened."

"Then we should dismiss him as lost to the white world and I will give away my daughter to someone else. I need to enjoy the fruits of having raised a daughter. I, too, like to eat from in-laws."

"Brother, please be patient. You are talking on behalf of Mungwi. How certain are you that she wishes to choose some other man? Girls today are different you know." Ba Daiga was close to the truth there. Before coming to Ba Daiga's home, Ba Tita had quarreled with his daughter and he knew her desires might be paramount.

He had said: "Mungwi, my daughter, do you know that you are growing out of marriage age? Why not look for some other man and get married instead of wasting your time and youthfulness waiting for a man you don't have any assurance is coming back to marry you?"

"No father. I can't do that until it is confirmed that Daiga is either married to someone else or dead."

"That is stupid, daughter. There is a saying in our tradition that when waiting for somebody on a journey, be advancing yourself, for you don't know in the long run whether he will make the journey with you at all."

"Father. I can't do that!"

"Then you pay me back all what I paid to your mother's father as dowry. For I see that you are prepared to make me lose everything I spent on your mother's father."

"I will when the time comes."

"I want to eat now not in years. You don't know when I am going to die."

That was the quarrel before Ba Tita set out to visit Ba Daiga. He even proposed to Ba Daiga to start paying the bride price before waiting for news of his son, but Ba Daiga said he could not possibly do that. There was actually a state of utmost confusion between the two families and Mungwi was the innocent sacrificial lamb while Daiga was more and more being seen as the culprit and instigator from afar. "Oh Lord, help me out of this mess. Tell me what is happening to Daiga over there in Germany. Advise me on what to do, dear Lord," Mungwi prayed. On top of this confusion suitor after suitor were leading her into temptation by offering themselves to her. Some of them were prosperous men who, to other than Mungwi, would have been hard to refuse.

There was this young district officer who came to her pleading: "I was presiding over the fundraising ceremony for the water project when my eyes landed on a cherubic face in the crowd. Since that day I have mounted a manhunt to find that face and figure. That face of that woman completely charmed me. Her figure gave me sleepless nights brooding about the possibilities of loving her infinitely. One particular day I asked God why he could not give me that woman as a wife. Finally God has allowed me meet you dear Mungwi. Give me your hand now. Be my darling wife. I promise I will love you forever."

"No," said Mungwi definitively "Someone came before you and I can't disappoint him."

"I have learned of this man you talk of. I hear he has been in Germany for over three years and is not corresponding with you or his parents. Some sources even hold that he is married to a German woman and has a child."

"All gossip. No one has proof of that," she insisted.

"My love, take my hand. We shall get married in the next few weeks. I shall refund all what Ba Daiga's family has spent. You know I am the district officer. A responsible figure like me should be married and not just to any woman. You are to me the first lady of the land. Please don't miss this chance in a million to be my wife."

"No," said Mungwi with firm determination.

"I swear to love you till the end of my days," he pleaded.

"No," was still Mungwi's response.

He was not the final suitor. There was also this smart young man who had made a fortune pirating books. He was not well educated but young, handsome and rich. He picked up approved school manuals published by foreign companies and skipped over to Nigeria to have them reprinted under the same cover and sold cheaper back in Cameroon. He was said to be making fabulous gains to the disadvantage of the original publishing house. He was fondly known among close collaborators as Jim Kikky. At age 30, he had two city buildings for his business and two well-furnished houses back in the village, each carrying parabolic dishes for television. He was the idol of villagers who admired prosperity. When he saw Mungwi he boasted: "Hey, don't you want to live in affluence with a tycoon like me?" Bragging of his wealth to every woman he approached usually turned them off and was why he was not married. "I have seven houses in my village each one carrying a parabolic dish and two Land Cruisers and I have 16 taxis plying different streets of the cities of Cameroon. I intend to buy a helicopter next year."

Mungwi was not taken in. "Maybe then you should go to a girl who is interested in helicopters and parabolic dishes for I am not interested in such things. I have already told you that I am promised to someone else."

"Engaged are you to someone in Germany? Maybe you don't know that what matters these days is not education and been-to-overseas, but money. If this guy comes home he will write an application to us to employ and pay him. We give jobs as drivers to some with doctorate degrees."

"No problem," said Mungwi. "Daiga will never come to you for a job."

Suitors came day in day out with their own stories to win Mungwi's hand. They were wasting their breath for Mungwi's heart was still with her chosen man far away in a different time zone and world.

Chapter 14

FREEDOM'S CALL

Though Daigo's relations with Monica were sliding down a slippery slope he was forging ahead in his political science classes. He had written an article for the student newspaper *Freedom* about his experience in East Berlin that was reprinted in the Stuttgart newspaper and for a time brought him a degree of notoriety from students and teachers gossiping in the pub and it even raised hilarity in upper university circles. The article was headed:

East Berlin functionaries arrested me

By Daiga

There I was, taking a walk along a quiet street in Mitte, East Berlin, with my wife and relatives, when plain-clothed men drew up in a car and arrested me.

I was driven through street after street, actually gaining sight of the Berlin Wall at one turn, until the vehicle screeched through a gate to a halt and I

*was marched into an interrogation room where an
East German interrogator questioned me mostly
in English about my conversation with one, Erich
Reuter, whom I had dined with that evening at the
home of my relatives.*

*Our main subject of conversation that I revealed,
first to my interrogator's dismay, then understanding
and finally humour was the prospective World Cup
football game between East Germany and my native
Cameroon…*

Daiga's article inspired a cartoon of an interrogator in red, black and gold strip missing a penalty goal on the football field kicked by Daiga. One result of the article was that Daiga was considering a request by the Stuttgart University student newspaper editor to join the board governing *Freedom* and another was that the *Stuttgart Zeitung* invited him to submit story ideas on German-African relations as a guest at an editorial meeting.

Daiga saw the two developments as being put there before him because he was a black African rather than a journalist so he declined both invitations as premature.

He was close enough to one of his professors, Herbert Mann, that when they went for a beer to discuss his progress in class he could break German university protocol by addressing him as Herbie. One evening, when the two were together in the university pub, the professor asked him: "So what is your aim in life, Daiga? Your progress insists that you make up your mind on your future. Africans are not successful in political careers or indeed in any public life here in West Germany. They are not fully accepted. I can't think of any who succeeded to high government echelon. We Germans are not fond of foreigners directing our lives. We have tended to direct theirs. That fault has cost us dearly. Do you intend to become a German citizen?"

"At first, when I served beer in this pub to make ends meet I thought that was my intent. No! I hope to return to Cameroon." Daiga burst out saying this without thinking he was revealing too much. "My future would be more secure in a small Cameroonian pool of intellects rather than in a large West German pool. The trouble is that Monica would not, could not, live in Cameroon. She is too German and in some ways her Jewish mother is anti-African. She fully accepts me as an underling within the family. At times her mother and daughter try to rule my life with an iron fist though Monica, like her father, can be outwardly gentle and understanding. She reminds me of the protagonist in the book you gave me to read. Remember, the German-language version of *Dr. Jekyll and Mr. Hyde* by Robert Louis Stevenson. The double exposure I see, more easily evident in photography than in my wife, depicts good and evil in man or woman. I wrote to a publisher in Edinburgh and now I have read the original English edition of Jekyll and Hyde too. There surely is good and evil in man and certainly also in woman. I am by no means saying Monica is evil. Just that this woman portrays some of the double exposures set out in Stevenson's book."

"Your analytical progress amazes me. Yet it also troubles me. Germans finally found out in World War II, via the route Adolf Hitler set us on, that evil can prevail over good. Stevenson's writing style does not translate easily into German. The Scotch words in some of his books are culturally confusing. It was from Stevenson that I learned the *pretty pickle* term. You apparently are in that pretty pickle with your marriage. Does returning to Cameroon not mean deserting Monica if she does not desire to go to Africa and deserting your son as well? You surely won't do that. It is strictly unethical. I think that by staying here in West Germany you might do well as a teacher. Why not teach English or French at elementary or high school? Was it not your original plan to be a teacher? West Germany needs teachers. You could very well succeed and in the long term save your marriage."

"No. Not really. Teaching was the career I set aside when I decided to continue at a higher level in your classroom. A good German elementary teacher acts almost like a father to his students. You have cut protocol by introducing this approach at university level. All your students have benefited from your interest in their problems. But you are made of sterner stuff than me. My past tells me I am not socially and instinctually good enough to be such a teacher. As to the future with Monica! I simply can't stay married to someone who will slowly destroy me. Teaching and my marriage have something in common there. As a teacher I would simply let down my students just as I am faced with letting her down because we are fundamentally different. Loving her has become impossible."

"Well, if not teaching, how about journalism? You made a good start with your article in *Freedom*. The whole university had a good laugh and the East Germans did not come out of it too badly. You could build on that to become a staff writer serving first the student newspaper and its board to gain experience. I don't know why you turned down their offer on the board. You could work your way up to editor to attract a Stuttgart or any other newspaper and find a niche at one of them as a political writer fluent in English, French and German and as an expert on Africa. Another idea is that with your looks and German language skills you could try for a career in what is fast-developing television journalism. A Canadian writer on television and advertising today says to both wide acclaim and just as wide discredit that the media is the message. You could be that message for the good of the world by bringing Africa to Europe at a time when winds of change are blowing. Multiculturalism is slowly growing in the world and you could boost it here in Germany."

"You think so. I doubt it. I say again that I could succeed easier as a diplomat or journalist in Cameroon where I believe newspapers need writers who show an understanding of world events. There is also a nascent television soon to come to the fore in Cameroon like it has for some time here in Germany. Its staff requires world knowledge. The needs of the African political world are similar almost all over the continent. For me those fundamental developments dictate that Cameroon will be the place for me."

"You know, Daiga, you really have improved intellectually since you first appeared in my class more than two years ago. You are more sophisticated and your mind more adroit. You have learned well. And one of the best of your attributes is that you know you have more to learn. Learning and doing are too different things. I am confident you could have a future here in Germany but you may be right to say Cameroon is the best place for you. For you even the sky may not be the limit there."

"I have family and friends in Cameroon. But more than that! I have a woman there who no doubt still awaits my promised return."

"Okay. That is a revelation to me. If then your marriage is breaking up because of promises or ties to another woman in Africa then you must face up to the inevitable. Remember though that you would be leaving your son behind. I know Monica somewhat. She would relentlessly oppose divorce or desertion. She loves you in her own Germanic way and might seek revenge in the way Hitler 35 years ago tried to avenge German humiliation at Versailles after World War I to almost everyone's doom including his own. I'm not exaggerating! You must know that Germans can be vengeful. Leaving Monica would leave you in the wrong because, after all, she is your wife and that will mean a lot to her. Give thought to the fact that she might seek to avenge desertion in one way or another. I warn you. Give good thought to it!"

"I promise," said Daiga. "Your advice is that of the thoughtful teacher I could never be." He then waved the student waiter over for two more beers hoping for more advice from a man he regarded as a brilliant humanist and friend.

"No more beer for me," Herbie declined standing up to leave. "I'm going home for dinner."

Daiga stood up to face him: "One important thing. You will look on our conversation as strictly confidential. I did not intend to shoulder you with so much of my personal life."

"I won't say a word."

"One other thing occurs to me. Should I leave suddenly for Cameroon would you in one way or another at one time or another in the future pass on this trinket to my son Burner?" Daiga handed over a tiny metal Cameroon flag he had taken from the lapel of his jacket. "Thanks a million professor. See you in class tomorrow."

Herbie for a moment stared down at the metal tricolore flag in the palm of his hand before saying: "This is a travesty. A trinket to replace a father! I'll gladly do what you ask if the occasion arrives but you need more advice. Why wait until tomorrow's class? We could continue our talk at my apartment tonight. I am on my own at home and I can make dinner for two unless of course you must go straight home to Monica."

It was an invitation Daiga could hardly refuse.

Chapter 15

DINNER FOR TWO

Herbie drove his red Porsche sports car far too fast. In next to no time he was showing Daiga into his penthouse suite located in an apartment block ten kilometres from the university.

The panoramic view from the living room window took Daiga's breath away and the wall of books on one side of the living room left him stunned. Herbie selected a book for him saying it was tough to read so it would certainly take up the time he would need in the kitchen rustling up dinner. The book, *The Medium is the Message,* was Herbie's choice. He reminded Daiga that this was the book he had referred to it in the pub.

Daiga cuddled down on a leather chesterfield and tried unsuccessfully to understand the meaning of its title. Then he read its first page. *"In a culture like ours, long accustomed to splitting and dividing all things as a means of control, it is sometimes a bit of a shock to be reminded that, in operational and practical fact, the medium is the message. This is merely to say that the personal and social consequences of any medium, that is, of any extension of us, results from the new scale that is introduced into our affairs by each extension of ourselves, or by any new technology."*

What did it mean? How could the medium be the message? Was he missing something? Who was this Canadian writer? What sort of a country was Canada? he asked himself thinking only of ice and snow. Since it was too much for him Daiga thought hilariously that maybe he would try this medium is the message out on Monica and see what she thought of it. He sat for 10 minutes silently trying to understand just that first passage.

His confusion was interrupted when Herbie emerged from the kitchen saying the food was nearly ready. "I'll try to explain McLuhan's message over the table in a few minutes. He's a devil to understand. I have been studying his work closely. I think it is mainly the new television news and advertising that has got him going on about the medium. I figured out that what he is saying is that control over change would seem to mean moving not with it, but ahead of it. Anticipation gives us the power to deflect and control force. Of course that is exactly what he is doing as well as driving me mad by making it so hard to understand for the reader to understand."

"I can understand that," Daiga commented, "but I would never have figured it out from what little I have read in half an hour."

"Well, McLuhan means what he says but, unfortunately, his meaning is not at all that obvious to the layman. Yes, he's hard to understand. I thought about trying to write a book clarifying his message. The problem is that I would end up stealing some of his ideas in simpler form. Doing that really *would* drive me mad and there would be no market for it here in Germany anyway."

Daiga thought the clearest thing he got from the McLuhan or Herbie messages was the hint that he would have to move ahead of his plan to return to Cameroon rather than be controlled by events or by Monica and her parents.

The table was set immaculately in the kitchen and the two sat down to spaghetti with meat sauce and salad, complemented by a Stuttgart Riesling and followed by apple strudel.

Daiga asked Herbie a question that had been on his mind for some time. "Why, in my political science classes, is the brutal aftermath of World War II rarely studied? It surely must be important for young Germans to learn about the war."

Herbie stroked his chin. Daiga was not the first student to have asked him this question. "The university believes the psychological import of World War II is too close to home and therefore dangerous for close study. Maybe it won't be the case in the distant future. German military tragedy and its aftermath are not political science. I would like to teach war history, but I am restrained by German war history. Frankly it is taboo."

"I would like to know more about what it was like living through World War II here in Germany," Daiga urged him on. "You must have been here at the time."

"Well, we have reminders like an article in the *Zeitung* on the same page as your article on your visit to East Berlin, your arrest by East German functionaries and your interrogation by an East German officer. Did you not see it? The article told how Albert Speer tried to save Berlin's several hundred beautiful Tiergarten trees in 1945 when the Red Army was charging madly into the city and artillery shells dropping.

"I must begin by telling you that Albert Speer, born around 1905, was Hitler's architect and for a while Minister of Production, bossing the economy of continental Europe during the Nazi power years in the early 1940s and before. At the war trials in Nuremberg he received a 15-20 year prison sentence after plausible deniability of criminal Nazi pursuits. He escaped the death sentence like presidents, kings and defence officials before him in history often have. Let me search my pile of newspapers to see if I can find the article. I kept it because not Speer but your article was important to me."

Herbie delved in a pile of newspapers in the corner of the room and came up with the *Zeitung* he was talking about.

"Here it is! You might be interested since you asked the question."

He cleared the dishes from the table and spread it out. "Let me explain a few important things first.

"Speer escaped the death sentences handed Hermann Goering and associates, although Goering escaped hanging by taking a potassium cyanide pill when he went to the toilet. It was presumed then that he had stuck the pill under chewing gum inside the toilet bowl. How would that have worked! In 1967, a final note he left said the pill was inside a jar of pomade. But here I digress. Anyway, Speer got 20 years in Spandau Prison in West Berlin, British sector, and Rudolph Hess, the fellow who flew to Scotland during the war, was given a life term.

"I will roughly translate for you conversations Speer had with 79-year-old Hans Baur, Hitler's personal pilot, as they appeared in *Zeitung* a week ago.

"They read: '*We were in front of the Brandenburg Gate as the Red Army was charging in. I was trying to get Speer's small Fieseler-Stork into the air. What did the lofty Herr*

Reichminister do? Speer spent one hour countermanding the orders that Hitler had given me to cut down a few hundred trees to clear runways for air emergency landings. There was Speer, frantically running up and down, grabbing axes from my hard working crew as my world was collapsing. The boy scout from the Palatinate in Bavaria had promoted himself to chief forester screaming out that he was the chief planner for Berlin and its post war construction.'"

Daiga held up a hand to stop Herbie in his tract. "Hold on! Are you telling me that this Speer fellow was trying to save some trees while Berlin, while Germany, was on the edge of an abyss at the hands of the Russians?"

"Yes! And I will tell you why and prove to you its truth."

"The article tells us that Speer, when released from prison recently, was walking down the Tiergarten on a bright autumn day when he was asked if the confrontation with Baur in1945 had actually occurred.

"According to the newspaper he replied: '*It was precisely the Berlin trees, those lindens, sycamores and elders that were important to me. A tree, even a war-blasted tree, is mankind's green symbol. It has roots in the past and spells hope for the future. It has taken Berlin 30 years to replace Baur's cutting in one hour. Perhaps we Germans, being forest people, have an ancestral thing about trees. It is certainly not our worst national quality.*

"'*A young man sits with a young woman under a tree. An old man plants trees although he knows he will never live to enjoy full shade or pick any fruit. Martin Luther once said that if God told him that the world would end in eight days he would go into the garden and plant an Apfelaeumchen, being a little apple tree.*'"

"Speer is reported to have continued: *'I am ashamed today of many things I did as Minister of the Third Reich, but not of my attempt to save those trees. For the future of Berlin even several hundred trees had become more important than the whole tawdry show at the Fuehrer Bunker.'"*

"So you see, I, as a professor here in Stuttgart, applaud and support Speer's defiance and would be happy teaching it. To end my discourse, Daiga, I can tell you that many of Berlin's Tiergarten trees today date from 1948-49. They were a gift from Queen Elizabeth of England and flown in as nursery trees by the Royal Air Force during the Berlin blockade. The British knew what had happened to the trees So you see, Daiga, good things can come out of bad things. We Germans are now ashamed of our criminal war pursuits and tend to keep quiet about them, but one could surely teach about Speer, the trees and the English queen, although it is more environmental or social than political science lessons."

Daiga searched for a word or two to say but he was mesmerized by his professor's stand. "You must have been a boy when World War II began and ended."

"I was 12 at the end and I must confess a member of the Hitler Youth. We were all members. Like Speer, I am not proud of my Nazi connection. I was lucky to escape recruitment into the German army at war's last fling. May I change the subject by asking if you would like coffee?"

"Shall I serve coffee or tea?" Herbie repeated the question louder while Daiga was thinking about the Hitler Youth.

"Okay," Daiga replied as his mind cleared.

"We will drink coffee in the living room. Sit back comfortably and I will serve you."

Daiga did as suggested and Herbie brought two steaming cups through on a tray, drew up a small table and sat down close beside him. "Am I not a good cook, Daiga?" he asked anticipating a positive reply.

"Best in Stuttgart, I would say."

"Are you comfortable?"

"Very!"

"Let me make you more comfortable then. "With those softly spoken words Herbie placed a hand on Daiga's knee and gently caressed it up and down staring intently at his handsome face. "Now instead of the medium being the message let me be the massage."

"What?" queried Daiga. "What did you say?" Daiga could not understand the change in Herbie from the professor he thought he knew to the seducer he never expected to know. He realized something was wrong and clamped down on the intrusive hand with his fist and with force pinned it to his thigh with his open hand.

Herbie first thought Daiga was encouraging him instead of holding him back retorted: "Free my hand!"

"Herbie, I have no respect for a man caressing me as if I were a woman. I'm not like that so stop it now. It is against the law I have a wife here and a fiancée in Cameroon. That should tell you that women attract me sexually but not sexy men."

"I have feelings for you, Daiga, can't you tell. These feelings took hold of me the day your classes began. They live within the heart of me yearning to be set free. Set yourself free from your women by hugging me instead of pinning my hand then stand up and take your jacket off! That will make us comfortable and you more receptive."

Daiga stood up in for a different reason. He recalled that Monica had once ordered him to do much the same thing. Herbie upright too ran a gentle hand down Daiga's cheek. "That is better. Now, do what I ask. Suits like the one you are wearing are made for professional work in public not for recreational endeavours in private."

"Herbie, you are out of your mind. You are homosexual. I don't believe what is happening."

"Do as I say, Daiga, or I will tell your wife you intend to leave her."

The threat shocked Daiga and the action of Herbie slowly unbuttoning his suit jacket and travelling with his hands a button too far while slipping one hand even further down set off an explosion within his brain.

"Stop!" he again shouted out. "I will not submit to homosexuality of any kind. What you are doing is taboo! You threaten me ignoring that I can get you thrown out of university by reporting this to the university authorities."

"What?" Herbie asked, curiously, raising his eyes level with Daiga's eyes. "It is love I seek not war. You wouldn't do that! The English poet Auden wrote that we must love one another or die."

"Homosexuality is not love it is a crime. Are you Jekyll or are you Hyde?"

Herbie's eyes narrowed and with a sheepish grin he replied: "Okay, you win. Your question is the winner. Maybe I have a split personality. There is a fine line between good and bad. We discussed that too. I was only fooling around with a handsome black fellow who had come to my apartment. I won't tell your wife a thing as long as you keep quiet about this silly adventure of mine. Button up your jacket. Buckle up.

Smile at my foolishness. Let us not make war. I'll drive you home. I solemnly promise that our future relations will be as professor to student. Take Marshall McLuhan's book home with you. I will be well rid of his global village rant!"

"The incident is forgotten," Daiga assured him. "You have my word for it. We have a deal not to harm each other."

"Peace in our time but not love. Is that your honest response?"

"Absolutely."

Chapter 16

INCOMMUNICADO

The deep cultural cracks in Daiga's marital relationship with Monica were inevitably increasing. When their Mercedes car had engine trouble, Monica quickly sold it without consulting him and put the money in her private rather than in their joint bank account funded by her father. This compelled him to travel by public transport and drive the Fiat only when he was driving her somewhere or when she was not using it. Daiga was not happy about this but he had no weapon to fight the humiliation he felt. Worse was when he came back from classes one day to learn that Monica's father had taken their son to Bonn to attend Jewish kindergarten there for a semester or two. There had been no consultation with him. Daiga got so cross that when he spoke he banged the table with his fist hard enough for a glass and plate to fall on the floor and shatter. "What right had your father or mother to do this?" he demanded, picking up the pieces.

"What is your problem? What do you do for them?" Monica replied picking up small broken pieces he had missed. "This will give him a better start to school and me some freedom to myself especially me when I am almost ready to continue university studies."

"He is my son and I must be consulted before any further decision is taken that affects him," Daiga retorted. "I gave in on his name, didn't I? I gave in on circumcision. What else does your mother require of me?"

"Any decision my parents or I take on Burner is best. You, as his father, must follow our lead. After all, what *do* you do for him? You earn no money and depend on my father financing you. My parents do everything and they love their grandson. They have the final decision on his schooling as well as his name. So speak of it no more."

Daiga knew the Wonkers had sponsored the child from birth: "It is true that your father has been very good to all of us. Was it your father, or was it your mother, who decided to send Burner to Jewish kindergarten in Bonn?"

"Actually, it was my idea thinking it might heal the break in our relations by giving us more personal freedom together."

Daiga wrestled with the complexity of an African man's traditional unchallenged control over the affairs of his home in Cameroon and what was transpiring around him in West Germany. He figured that from his point of view rather than contributing to freedom for the two of them his wife was really contributing to the breakdown of their marriage. For five weeks Monica and he at his insistence had slept in different rooms because their problems were becoming less pleasant each day. She would tactfully or demandingly domineer and he would resist weakly or try to hit back. To Daiga she seemed to have more strength of character than he had and would always hit hard by saying he was contributing nothing in monetary terms to their lives,

She had insisted he attend synagogue with her and to his dismay hinted he should respect more her Jewish faith. "I did not think you were such a follower of Zionism," he had thoughtlessly replied.

"That is insulting. I see you are really angry with me but you must not at the same time insult me. I tell you these manifestations of yours will never solve our marriage problems. Before we came together I reminded you that I was a girl of European not African culture. You accepted that and you must live with it. Our differences are not insoluble. Maybe you are thinking that your wife is wicked in some of her ways. Monica is not wicked. She loves you. Come back to our marital bed and make me happy. Let us forge ahead with our marriage vows. That is how things should be." Having said this she had tried to kiss Daiga, but he had pushed her away as their lips met. Things were so bad that her actions had even begun to remind him of the foolishly homosexual way Herbie had acted. When had he insulted her Jewish faith? He wondered how many Germans were like her in alleging untruths. Had pseudo-romanticism, dogmatism and civil domination replaced German militarism?

"Well, have it your own damned stupid way!" she exclaimed when her lips missed his lips.

He pondered over what she had said: *"Have it your own damned stupid way."* And before that: *"This is how things should be."*

Now he was certain it would be wise of him to leave Germany for Cameroon before he became a total Jewish poodle. His son had been taken from him no doubt by his grandmother on grounds of Jewish schooling and no doubt circumcised for reasons beyond the child and himself. Daiga inwardly exclaimed the word abomination. For him to play a secondary role to two women was unthinkable in the African if not the European context. It could not continue. A vision of Mungwi appeared in his mind. Leaving Monica sitting alone he went to his study and picked up pen and paper.

"My darling Mungwi,

I know you will be thinking that I have abandoned you. It is not exactly what you may think. It is because of studies. Maybe I should inform you that I went in for a full degree course in political science at the University of Stuttgart. I shall be taking my Bachelor of Arts exam in July this year and I shall return home thereafter to make arrangements for our marriage if you are still available to me and compete for a job with the Cameroon government. Please, in the name of love, forgive me a hundred times, for I am a sinner."

Foncham Daiga.

He folded his letter into an envelope with a stamp and addressed it. Monica was using a feather duster in the sitting room when she saw him cross past her with the envelope in his hand. She rushed to the window to see him walk to the street postal box and mail it. Who could Daiga be writing to just after their quarrel? Daiga rarely received or sent letters to or from anybody to the best of Monica's knowledge. To Monica this particular letter was suspicious. So suspicious she vowed to do everything possible to learn its details. In a few minutes Daiga was back without the envelope.

"You mailed a letter. Who are you corresponding with?" she asked bluntly as he was crossing back to his study.

"No-one important and anyway it's none of your businesses," replied Daiga, happy to frontally avenge his felt lack of independence with strong words. She smiled and continued her dusting. But in her mind she swore she would do everything to know the recipient of her husband's letter.

"You take up too much time inquiring into my personal life," he added from his study door. "You need something to fill your time. I have purchased a book by a Canadian author for you to read. Let me know what you think of it."

Monica was impressed with the gift from her husband. "Well. Thank you." Thinking he might respond to her thanks with an embrace she moved closer toward him. Daiga promptly turned on his heels and returned to his study to work on a dissertation towards his degree. They continued to live virtually incommunicado as Daiga busily prepared to defend his thesis and plan his escape.

As luck would have it, Daiga's thesis was deemed complete on the first draft to an internal committee. The final step to defend it before the committee and an external adviser duly arrived.

Daiga entered the adviser's office and was impressed with the welcome given him by a seemingly warm, kind examiner who handed him a sheet of questions he would verbally put to him. Daiga read through them as he was advised. Suddenly question four jumped off the pages and hit him squarely between the eyes. He felt a nervous shake around his shoulders. Before him was a question that identified a fundamental political flaw in his thesis that both he and the entire committee had missed and that simply could not be defended by the data he had drawn up.

He took the unusual action of excusing himself and going to the sanctuary of the men's washroom to reflect and analyze an answer. He first thought that he was faced with an ethical dilemma that could change the direction of his life. He saw that he was entirely on his own in seeking a solution.

Daiga knew he could not reflect on the problem any length of time by himself in the washroom. His external adviser might smell a rat. He decided that his best defence was honesty and integrity. Nothing would be gained by trying to bullshit his way out by defending an error.

He entered the adviser's office calm in the knowledge he would do the right thing. Exactly as promised his external adviser proceeded one by one asking the questions he had indicated. Question 4 was asked and Daiga, after a brief pause, responded: "You are right. This shows a flaw in my thesis that I shall be totally aware of in future." With hardly five seconds of hesitation the examiner with a smile of approval moved on to the next question. There were no more traces of error in Daiga's answers. He later congratulated himself in winning his degree by guile worthy of a real master.

Chapter 17

LETTER FROM STUTTGART

This blessed day in Cameroon was a day in April when the rains had filled the potholes in Ntoafoang roads with muddy water. There was no escaping a Renault, with a foreign license plate, that swept by pedestrians at terrific speed for the conditions, splashing the mud on everyone walking by the roadside. Mungwi was one of the people who had her dress messed up by the speeding car. She had worked at the farm all day changing into a clean dress for her return home and she was cross with whoever the driver was. Fifty metres ahead the driver realized what he had done and backed up to Mungwi and others. She was fuming and would not listen to his apologies for she had a long way to go home in a dirty dress. The driver, seeing no other way to appease her, proposed he drive her home. She readily accepted in view of the mess of mud on her dress.

"What about the others," she pointedly asked.

"I can't drive everyone home."

Dropping her at her compound entrance, he asked: "Who is my unfortunate but lucky passenger?"

"My name is Mungwi," she told him. "Does my dress indicate I am lucky?"

"I am the new postmaster for the district post office here and I consider you lucky to get a drive home," the man told her repeating her name again and again.

"Mungwi Tita? Looks like I saw a letter in today's mail bearing that name."

"No, impossible," declared Mungwi, hurrying to take her leave thinking it one of those fancy men's ploys to detain her and start talking rubbish to her. "It cannot be true."

"I swear I saw *that* name. I sorted the letters myself today because my staff were on break by the time the letters came. I particularly remember that one because it was erroneously put with the letters for Batibo and I discovered it only after cross-checking the bags."

Mungwi was still not convinced.

"I am not expecting a letter from anyone," she maintained with the intention of leaving him seated in his car. She moved off, but stopped to look round when the man said: "Have you someone you know in Europe? This letter carries a foreign stamp, French, or was it German?"

"German!" Mungwi excitedly broke in with steps back in his direction.

"Yes, more likely from Germany. You have someone in Germany you know. There you are then. There's a letter for you from Germany."

"Can I get it now?" she asked, her excitement growing. She had always kept hopes alive that Daiga would come back to her.

"Let's go to the post office. I am the postmaster. I can open the boxes at any time."

"Yes, let's go," Mungwi said with excitement all over her face.

They drove to the district post office where the postmaster opened a box and searched among letters. Mungwi's heart beat harder with anticipation and excitement that had taken hold of her. Could this man be wrong? If so how come he had pinpointed Germany? After about two minutes of rummaging the man pulled out an envelope with handwriting Mungwi knew well. It was neatly addressed to Miss Mungwi Tita. Her heart pounded harder. Would it be Daiga telling her he was married and that she should look for someone else? Or could it be good news? With quivering fingers she tore open the envelope and there and then read its contents."

"I will come back and marry you!" She almost said the most important words aloud but the postmaster was close by.

"You look happy. Who is it? Is it a relative or friend in Germany?"

"It is from a friend," she replied thanking him and taking off for home. She ran into her compound shouting: "Mother, father, mother, father, Daiga is coming back!" Her cries drew villagers out to see the letter from Germany that she was waving in the air.

"That is good my daughter," said her father. "I am going to Ba Daiga's house right away to discuss the different items of the dowry."

"Father! You have not even rejoiced with your daughter over the good news. All you think of is the bride price and your stomach."

"That is where my memory is." With that said he went direct to Ba Daiga's compound.

"My brother," Ba Daiga asked when Ba Tita broke the news to him "are you really saying that my son wrote your daughter saying that he is coming home?"

"I saw the letter with my own eyes even though I cannot read. I don't think my child deceives me. She said he is coming home with his big certificate that he has learnt from the white man's land. But now I forget exactly what else I come to tell you." Ba Tita soon remembered he had come to enumerate the items for the bride price. "You know you have to pay exactly the same items I paid for her mother and even more because I have educated her up to high school."

"That is no problem my brother. If we are lucky enough to have Daiga back to avert a major embarrassment what is money to again pay all that you ask of us?"

While this was going on at Ba Daiga's house, Mungwi was replying to Daiga's letter.

Darling,

I did not believe my eyes when I heard from you again after all those years. Especially that you were coming back in July to marry me. I look forward to your return with impatience touched by anxiety. What sins you committed will be tossed aside as testimony to our love.

Your Mungwi, forever.

She rushed to the store, bought an envelope and addressed it to:

Daiga Foncham

75 Kernestrasse

Stuttgart, West Germany, and put it in her handbag with the short letter inside. Early next morning she was back at the post office where she purchased stamps, fixed them on the envelope and dropped it in the postal box.

Chapter 18

THE POSTMAN RINGS

It was by then May in Stuttgart and Daiga was feeling more and more bored with life in Germany from the food, the cold spring weather and the professors to even German men and women generally and he was glad he had avoided the *Stuttgart Zeitung* board room. He no more wanted anything German, most of all he did not want Monica, whom he fervently wished to discard in the shortest possible time. He needed Cameroon food such as fufu and jamajama to fill up his taste sense. He yearned for African village environment, natural people and woman like Mungwi with her delicate feminine ways. August would not see him in Stuttgart he vowed. He was not at home on the day the postman came to drop mail in their home box. Maybe his presence would have averted a potentially major crisis for him.

Monica was alone when the doorbell rang. The postman was not used to ringing the bell. He usually just put the mail in the box each time he brought it. What made him decide to hand the mail that day straight into someone's hands only God alone knew?

Monica was handed the envelopes and scrutinized them. Two were from phone and electricity companies carrying consumption bills for that month and one from her mother in Bonn. A fourth envelope aroused her curiosity. It was addressed to Daiga Foncham. Carefully opening it without tearing the envelope and glancing at the bottom of the short letter to see who had sent it she winced when she saw *Your Mungwi, forever.*

She shifted to the nearest chair and sat down to study what she saw as a note rather than a letter. Then she nodded. Obviously it was a reply to the letter Daiga had posted the previous month. Beautiful catch, she thought. When she had decided what to do with it she opened one of the drawers to her cupboard in the dressing room she alone used, placed the letter in it, locked the cupboard and dropped the key into her handbag.

When Daiga came home Monica welcomed him with an embrace as though nothing was wrong. She served him lasagna for dinner and asked how he had found his studies that day.

"Fine, no problem," answered Daiga, wondering if her welcome meant she was up to something fishy.

He had written to Mungwi in April. It was now June and he still had received no word back. This worried him. Had Mungwi thrown his words of love and admission of sin out to the sin bin and married someone else? God forbid it! He did not want to go through a difficult and embarrassing process of making a choice out of the many other girls back home to replace Mungwi. He wanted just her. He wanted no woman who might turn out to be another Monica. He had looked in the post box each day on returning from the university to see if there was a letter from Mungwi. Most of the mail received during the years he had been with Monica was official mail addressed to both of them that Monica never cared to read and was placed on his reading table. Little did he suspect that Monica would open mail addressed directly to him. He still believed in her to that extent. He simply had accepted that Mungwi had not replied. One day, in the faculty, he decided to write her another letter. He picked up paper and pen and wrote:

Hi Dear,

What has happened that you have not replied to my letter? Please, even if you are unavailable for me now for one reason or another, just reply to let me be aware before I return in August with my degree in political science.

Love,
from your Daiga Foncham.

He folded the letter, pushed it in an envelope and addressed it to Mungwi. On the other side he wrote: *"If not available return to ...* just by instinct as he was writing he cast his eyes on the faculty notice board and read the faculty postal box address and asked himself why not start receiving his mail there. He wrote, *Daiga Foncham, Faculty of Political Sciences, private 87 PO Box 19, University of Stuttgart, West Germany,* on the envelope, then walked over to the faculty post office, stuck stamps on the envelope and dropped it in the post box.

When he returned home that night he unexpectedly received what he thought of as a boring and insipid sudden welcome kiss from Monica, went straight to his study and picked up some newspapers that she had dropped on his table. He flipped through their contents, threw them on a corner pile, leaned back on his chair contemplating the end of course activities, his planned arrival home and his wedding to Mungwi should she tell him she was still available. He picked up a small pocket diary from the table, opened it on the July page, and wrote:

July 20th: Return to Cameroon.
July 21st: Arrival at Douala Airport
July 22nd: Arrival in Bali
August: Marriage arrangements
September 21st: Proposed wedding day

After that he pocketed the diary, picked up a sheet of paper and roughly drafted what he expected the wedding invitation would look like. Writing down his timetable to Daiga seemed to him a dream come true that he was back in Cameroon.

Wedding bells

The families of Ba Daiga and Ba Tita
are pleased to invite the company of Hon. Dr. Rev.
Mr. Mrs. Miss------------------------------ to the
nuptial ceremony of their son and daughter, Daiga
Foncham and Mungwi Tita, on 21st September at the
Presbyterian Church, Ntafoang, at 2 p.m. prompt. A
wedding party shall immediately follow at the Bali
Community hall.

RSVP.

When he was still deciding what names would feature on the RSVP section the doorbell disturbed him. He tried to ignore it, but it insisted.

"Monica, Monica! Someone is at the door. Kindly attend please," he called out, but Monica was not responding and the doorbell continued to disturb him. He carelessly left the invitation on the table and went to attend to any intruding party. It was the mechanic with their Fiat he had been working on all day. Daiga opened the bonnet and inspected the work done on the engine as if he knew something about it.

"Perfect," he said. "Can I try it out and so drop you at the garage?" The mechanic readily accepted the offer and off they went.

Monica, who had been trimming thorns on the roses in the back yard garden, turned round to see the car move off. "Is it the car?" she yelled, thinking Daiga was still in his study. No one answered. "Daiga! Daiga!" she called out.

Still not getting an answer she moved to the study to check on him. Daiga was not there of course, but the note on the table caught her eye. It looked like a note for her, lying with pen on paper. She picked it up and read Daiga's wedding invitation. "Daiga and Mungwi. Perfect catch!" she exclaimed in alarm and gratitude for her discovery. She placed the note against her chest, looked up and spoke out loud to herself: "Thank you, God, for this revelation of betrayal." She went to the photocopy machine in the sitting room, photocopied the note and placed the duplicate in her private drawer. She returned the draft to its original position on the table and placed the pen on it as if no one had touched it.

Daiga drove back after 15 minutes, made straight for the study and closing the door behind him sat down to again read the invitation he had drafted. He approved the draft and pushed it into his student file to work with it more carefully and freely when he went to the faculty room the next day. Three weeks later he received a reply from Mungwi that delighted him. All was well with her. She was waiting impatiently for his return.

Mungwi had used the faculty address this time and the letter came straight to Daiga. She also advised Daiga to write out a proposed program of activities. This was exactly what he had already done so he simply removed his pocket diary, copied down the program he had drafted and took it to the computer room to give it to the faculty typist who neatly typed it out on the computer keyboard and printed it for him. One person was sitting close by but Daiga did not know or care who she was. He just folded the typist's work, put it in an envelope, addressed and stamped it and left to mail it to Mungwi.

While Daiga was mailing his July program to Mungwi something unknown to him was happening in the computer room. The woman who had been sitting waiting for the computer to free up so that she could print out her thesis had cast her eyes on the screen he was using. She spoke to the faculty typist who confirmed what she thought. What had captured her attention were the return to Cameroon and the wedding date. She closed her eyes, leaned back, and tried to remember where she had known this guy."

"Oh yes! Was this not her friend Monica's husband Daiga?" she reminisced Why was he talking about returning to Cameroon in July and being married in September? Did it mean Monica would be going to have a second marriage ceremony there? If so that was news to her. Why would Monica choose to wed in Cameroon when as far as she knew she and her husband had everything going for them in Stuttgart? She decided to talk to Monica and find out if she had really taken such a decision. She fitted a 25 pfennigs piece in a public phone and dialed Monica's number.

"Hi, frau, it's Marla here. Don't tell me you and Daiga are going to Cameroon to wed again?"

Monica, from the other end, stammered: "You… you are asking me what?"

"Don't tell me you want to hide it. Your return wedding program for July and August was in the computer in front of me. Your husband had it printed out at the faculty office."

"Oh, Daiga is so kind," Monica said, recovering her wits. "I never knew he was going to do that for me. The guy is a darling. Is he still there?"

"No, he just left."

"Please kindly tell the computer girl to print out three copies for me. I shall be there in 20 minutes to pick them up. I may send copies to relatives. Thanks Marla."

In 20 minutes Monica had picked up copies of the program. Back home she placed them in the drawer beside the other papers and locked them up. When Daiga returned she behaved as though she was without a care in the world. She had seen through him and planned to act at the right time.

Chapter 19

THE ROOT OF EVIL?

Mr. Wonker, though a rich tycoon, was a Jewish gentleman of good faith and good intentions. He sincerely wished the best for his children and grandchild. He believed children such as his had the right to enjoy paternal wealth such as his. He loved Monica and to an extent admired Daiga whom he hoped soon to help out with a job. He saw Daiga as progressing well at university. He especially appreciated that they had given him the grandson he occasionally cradled on his knees.

He had pleaded with Monica to withdraw from university for one year to give the baby a safe upbringing and had made the arrangements to pay for their home and living costs while Daiga studied. Monica accepted all this but told her father she now needed time to plan *her* studies. Mr. Wonker had continued to send them a cheque every three months. It was enough money to run the home and pay for Daiga's academic expenses until the next cheque arrived. Mr. Wonker also sent money for rent at the beginning of each year. He had opened an account for them at the Sud West bank where he deposited a cheque in Bonn for them to draw money on in Stuttgart. Mr.

Wonker just wrote on his cheque, The Daigas, and below he wrote Monica and Foncham Daiga. This meant that either of them could draw money from the account. The next cheque was due in July for rent and for three months of expenses. Little did Mr. Wonker know about the biblical notion that love of money could be the root of all evil as it was about to turn out.

Daiga was planning his future away from his wife and out of West Germany. He took his return air ticket to the Air France agency to confirm the ticket was still valid for return to Cameroon after four years. He discovered it was not. He had in the circumstances one vital thing to do. If he could cash in his father in law's cheque from Bonn, clearing the equivalent of about five million francs in Cameroonian currency, it would pay for his airfare, a royal wedding in Cameroon, a car for the honeymoon and leave enough money to support Mungwi and himself until he picked up a job with the Cameroon government.

Knowing nothing of this Monica planned to keep Daiga deprived of travel documents to the extent she could until the day she would mightily surprise him face to face with the details of his secret plan to leave her. She went to the Sud West bank and asked to talk to the manager.

"What can I do for you?" the manager asked. "Do you need some financial assistance?"

"No," said Monica. "I just want you to protect our family account."

"What is up?" the manager asked. "Your money is protected by the bank."

"I just wish to be cautious," she said showing her usual discretion about naming names. Monica was the kind of woman who rarely washed dirty linen in public.

"Who do you suspect could try to play smart on your account?" asked the manager focusing his eyes on Monica over his lenses and trying to draw her out.

"Just anybody," she said.

"Okay. I will do just that. I will call you if I find anything suspicious."

"Thank you, sir. I count on your diligence."

With this precaution taken Monica knew that if she got hold of Daiga's Cameroonian passport he would be straitjacketed at home in West Germany. Without money and travel documents he would be virtually cut off from the outside world and rightly humbled. Life would then continue as normal with her in charge until she faced him with the positive evidence of his intended desertion.

Back home she went into Daiga's room and rummaged his drawers. It paid off. She found two travel documents, placed them in her private drawer and locked it. She celebrated with a glass of whisky and vowed in a fit of anger that, if she could not do so, her father would deal with Daiga.

Chapter 20

HIDDEN PLANS

Thousands of kilometers away in Cameroon, Mungwi went to the parish minister and booked a wedding for September 21. She had to register the wedding at least two months in advance so that the announcement allowed for opposition and ample time for any necessary solution. Then she sent a copy of the wedding announcement to the council for publication. With this done she wrote a letter to Daiga telling him that everyone was set to receive him at the Douala airport and at Bali. Important wedding arrangements had been made. The airport rendezvous was to be on July 21 at 9 a.m.

Mungwi, erroneously thinking that since it was June 28 schools in Germany would be on holiday as was the case in Cameroon, where schools closed for summer holidays by mid June, addressed the letter to Daiga's home and dropped it in the post office.

A week later, in Stuttgart, her letter again went straight into Monica's hands. She smiled when she read it. Black monkeys didn't know anything. She would shatter Daiga's dreams just before he was to leave and teach him a lesson he would never forget. He would surely have to remain in Germany when everything had been exposed to her father about his plan to desert her and found he had no money or travel documents. If not her father would see to it that Daiga was taken to task.

On July 16, Monica and a few family friends accompanied Daiga to the university to learn he had been awarded first class honours. Graduation day was named and Daiga noted it carefully on the calendar.

It was a lovely summer's day when he lined up for the formal presentation in the university hall. Also present from Bonn were Monica's parents. Daiga strode onto the platform in his best suit and bowed to the university president who tapped him on the shoulder and handed him his testimonial with a word of congratulations.

Students and their friends assembled in the university gardens to talk and enjoy tea and sandwiches. "Well, you did it," Mr. Wonker said warmly to Daiga. "I now have ideas for your advancement through my contacts with a business school in Bonn. With three languages and a Master's degree the sky is the limit."

"Yes, you have it right. Mr.Wonker, I presume," a voice broke in from nearby. It was that of Professor Herbert Mann, who had come over to congratulate Daiga and had overheard the conversation.

Daiga introduced him to the family. "Professor Mann has kept me right for three years I owe this day to this wonderful teacher."

"No, Daiga, you owe your success to yourself and your wonderful wife who has kept in the background while you pursued your studies. You may remember me, Monica, as one who spoke at your high school leaving ceremony and presented you with a prize for German essay I believe it was."

Monica blushed at the compliment. "I just told my father that it is now my turn to study for a degree. I hope you will be my teacher formally or otherwise."

"A pleasure I could never have hoped to be rewarded with."

Professor Mann further coloured her face by kissing her hand. "Daiga must be as proud of you as you are of him."

Daiga smiled with caution wondering what Herbie was up to if anything more than polite conversation. He wondered if the professor had designs on a rich wife about to be discarded by him. He had learned that Herbie was in financial difficulties through poor investments on the stock exchange and had sold his Porsche and moved out of his expensive apartment. "You are too good," he told the professor politely, putting a traitorous arm around Monica as if he really was proud of her.

Daiga kept hidden deep down within his soul his plan to leave West Germany for a civil service job in the Ministry of Foreign Affairs in Cameroon and to marry Mungwi. If Herbie fancied Monica he would gladly give her to him. The rub was that knowing that Herbie was the only person who knew of his plan to desert her had made him nervous of disclosure if his wife and he became friends.

Monica hid her intention to expose Daiga's planned desertion and scuttle his departure almost on the airport runway. She did not intend to rock the boat just yet. She was determined by all means at her disposal to have him miss the plane after which she would threaten to expose him publicly for his betrayal unless he crawled back to her bed and pledged never to leave again.

Totally unaware of the devilishly-laid schemes lurking below the surface, Mr. Wonker announced that a celebratory dinner was in store that night for Daiga. "We will find the best restaurant in Stuttgart and the best bottle of wine on the Schilelrplatz to raise a toast to my remarkable son so that each of us will remember this special day. Will you join us Professor Mann?"

Chapter 21

WHERE IS DAIGA?

Early the following week Monica returned home from her hairdresser just minutes after Daiga had broken into her locked drawer and fled the house. Nothing prompted her on her return to move directly into her bedroom. Hungry, she instead went into the kitchen to prepare potatoes in a traditional German cabbage soup with croutons. This took her the best part of an hour. When finished she placed it on top of a warm plate on the dining table and lit a candle intending to eat with her husband when he returned home.

She was still waiting for Daiga at 6 p.m. so she ate alone. She wondered what could possibly have kept him so long. Then she figured he might have had to go to the university to pick up his attestation. She decided to go into Daiga's study to see if by chance he had already brought home his testimonial and perhaps left it on his desk before going out. On entering she was astonished to discover his belongings scattered everywhere. Everything in his room was lying around. Bags and boxes were overturned, drawers and cupboards wide open. Surely Daiga had been searching for something. Could it have been his travel documents? She quickly ran to her bedroom to make sure that they were safe in her locked drawer. At that moment she noticed that the door of her bedroom was not fully closed. This alarmed her because she rarely left her door open and she alone now used the room. Her heart beat faster. Had Daiga been in her room? On entering, she cast her eyes on the bedside cupboard drawer and sat down on the bed in shock after realizing it had been broken into and the contents taken.

So Daiga had found his letters and documents. She put her left thumb between her teeth and gently bit it. One thing she was fairly sure of was that Daiga had no yet left the country. His flight was on the 20th of July and that day was only the 18th. Moreover she doubted he had the money to buy an airline ticket. Or was he hiding in the city possibly making plans to get his old return air ticket, she knew he held, upgraded for his flight on the 20th?

She lay back to contemplate what to do if that was what he was up to. She concluded in alarm that Daiga would likely not come back home at all having left it in such a mess. He would surely be squatting with someone. It occurred to her that Daiga might try to get money from the family account. She searched her bag, got out her telephone address booklet and picked up the phone receiver to call the bank.

"What's wrong with this phone?" she frustratedly asked herself putting it to her ear a second time. There was still no dial tone. "Bother!" she exclaimed planking the receiver down and dashing out of the house to the public phone. The bank had closed so her call rang unanswered. Then she started calling everyone of good standing who might know where Daiga was.

"Did you see my husband today? I haven't seen him since this afternoon. I just wish to find out what could have kept him out all day and if he is okay."

No one had seen him. Satisfied that she had contacted every person that could be keeping Daiga hidden, she decided she would alert the bank manager first thing in the morning to play safe with her account. This time she would tell the manager that the danger to her money was none other than her husband and that he should not sign out any money to him.

Daiga was surely going to find he was near penniless and come crawling home on his hands and knees. All of a sudden she realized that Professor Mann might know her husband's whereabouts. She again dashed out to the phone because it was getting late. Her call caught him almost going to bed. "I have sad news for you Monica. I fear he has deserted his family and gone home to Cameroon," he replied on being told Daiga was missing and asked if he knew where he was.

"But his home is here. So you knew he intended to desert me?"

"Yes, he told me so."

"But he can't have gone yet. He is booked to leave in two days."

"So you knew too."

"I intend to stop him at the airport and expose what is a matrimonial crime."

"Monica, don't be silly. I will come over to your apartment to console and advise you. I fear Daiga has tricked you and left you for his real home and his real woman."

Monica broke down crying at the words coming from Daiga's teacher.

"I am his wife. Am I not his real woman?" she sobbed.

"You have to realize that culturally Daiga and you come from two different worlds…"

Monica crashed down the telephone in fury wondering why the professor was not on her side. She had her first doubts that Daiga was still in Stuttgart. Yet she had solid evidence that indicated he was due to leave for Cameroon in two days.

Early next morning she again went to the public phone booth and stood there for 15 minutes waiting for bank opening hours. She was sure that by 8.30 a.m. the manager would he in his office. At that hour she called and told him: "This is Monica of account No. 300198. I wish to reiterate what I told you the other day. The dangerous element is none other than my husband Daiga. If he comes asking for money from our account don't give him any." Then she heard the manager make a deep mumble of, "Oh, my god!"

"Is anything the matter?" she asked.

"Maybe," said the manager indicating to her that he was hiding something. "Can you come over to the bank so that we can talk this over? There may be repercussions."

Monica did not need a god in heaven to tell her that the manager's reaction meant that Daiga had been to the bank.

"How much has he withdrawn?" she bluntly asked.

"Everything in your joint account which I suppose he has a claim to. With the intention of paying bills and going on holiday with you."

Monica was stunned but could not blame the manager when the fault was hers. She had not put the bank manager fully in the picture when she earlier in the week had warned him to take care of her account. So he had withdrawn all their money. She thought how lucky she was to have a separate account of her own with some of her father's money in it. Was Daiga still in Stuttgart? His flight was not due to leave until the next day. He had put that day in his program so he surely planned to leave that day. Monica was not quite totally confused. No use going to the bank manager again. The damage had been done. The better decision was to check the flight schedule at the airport and trap him there for being the criminal he was or for the crime he intended. She conjured with a citizen's arrest at the airport. She discarded that idea and instead opened the city telephone directory, found the number of the Lufthansa Air Company, dialed, and asked: "I wish to know how and when one would get a flight for Douala, Cameroon." The man at the other end told her that Lufthansa did not fly to Douala and that she could try Air France. When she dialed Air France the man told her that such a flight took off twice a week late in the evening with transit at Paris and that the next flight for that week was on Friday, July 20, in fact, the next evening, but that it was fully booked.

Monica was sure Daiga must have reserved a place on that flight as he had planned and would be taking off from Stuttgart the next day. He was surely planning to respect his outlined program to meet his family and fiancée in Douala as stated in their correspondence. This annoyed her all the more. All this jubilation in Cameroon would be at her and her father's expense and she had not disclosed the theft to him. No, his desertion must not be permitted. She crossed back into her house, sought out money, put it in her handbag and caught the airport bus. She first studied the airport entrance and parking where vehicles and taxis dropped passengers. Then she went to the waiting rooms and studied them. There were three in all. She determined where one could sit and watch passengers coming in without being conspicuous.

Satisfied with her findings she went straight to the Lufthansa Airlines desk and booked a return flight to Bonn. She boarded the plane and arrived in Bonn in the afternoon. Her father came back for his usual late lunchtime break to meet her. "Hi Monica," he called out in surprise. "You didn't tell me you were coming."

"Just came to see my son and ask you for a favour," she said.

"He will be out with your mother in the park. "What favour can I offer you?"

"Father, I need a gun."

"A gun!" exclaimed a further surprised Mr. Wonker "What for?"

"For self-defence," Monica lied. "As you know the Baader-Meinhof trial is underway near Stuttgart and university students have been alerted to watch their step. There is support for the Red Army Faction among left-wing students and my point is that they don't like Jews. They say the trial may go on for a long time and may put students at risk."

"Yes, I know about the trial. Surely that anti-West trash is not targeting you," her father said leaning forward to look with concern into Monica's eyes.

"Not exactly," she replied trying to appear calm rather than jittery. "But you never realize you need a gun until the moment you are surprised and it is too late. I really would feel safer armed."

"Does Daiga know you wish to arm yourself with a gun?"

"No."

"Oh, I see," said Mr. Wonker, thoughtfully thinking he would ask Daiga about that when he got the chance. "But because of your age and gender you know you need some kind of a special license before carrying a gun. Giving you a gun is not the problem."

"I can surely get a license after I get the gun. I can't train without a gun."

"But you must assure me that you need a gun for only self-defence and that you are not hiding anything. I don't want to see you run into trouble with the law or with Daiga. If you assure me of that, I can give you a gun. After all, I have three good revolvers at your disposal."

"There is no problem with Daiga or the law. It is for my personal safety during the trial period. I will apply for a license immediately I return to Stuttgart and I will take a firearms course."

Mr. Wonker went into his back room and brought out a .45 calibre. "If you feel you really must have a gun, this is what I can offer you. It is a close range shooter to be used only when you are really in trouble and when the target is less than 20 metres away. The magazine carries five bullets with automatic firing power if its use becomes necessary to defend yourself."

He drew out the magazine and showed Monica the bullets lined up around a small wheel. If you are not firing automatically then you must drag up the trigger each time you fire in order to release the bullet. For automatic firing you push this button to the left. You continue pulling the trigger and the magazine will rotate and empty of bullets. Now that you have this gun above all be careful not to accidentally do anything nasty and on no account enter into any political argument. And remember to keep this safety catch on and the gun locked away when it is not in use. I advise you to discuss your fears with Daiga, but do not give him the gun. When the emergency atmosphere improves you must immediately give this gun back to me. I repeat that you must not let a soul know you have a gun."

"Thanks father. I will be careful not to do anything stupid. The object temporarily is safety first in an emergency."

The day was Thursday, January 19. She was in a hurry to return home and there were regular flights to Stuttgart from Bonn. She shrewdly picked up a few food items from a grocery store, bought a grocery bag and outside the shop placed the gun at the bottom of the bag below her groceries. With the gun out of sight she took a taxi to the airport. Lucky for her the German airport authorities did not mount serious searches of hand luggage on local flights. She passed through airport security and soon was home in Stuttgart.

In her room she removed the gun, inspected it and spoke half dementedly to herself in a mirror. "I am no more your Monica of when we first met. I am the white devil coming to get the black betrayer."

She put the gun in her handbag, placed her handbag in a cupboard and bedded down. Sleep did not come easily. Her mind revolved over which part of Daiga's body she would hit with a bullet at the airport. Would it be face, chest or belly? She decided it didn't matter where she shot him as long as she killed or maimed him. The type of execution mattered little to her. Daiga had already executed her. What would her friends think? Most important was how her son would fare with no father and a mother guilty of killing him if the situation reached a last resort. And how would her father explain to their son his loss of parents if worse came to worst?

Her thoughts turned sleep into a nightmare in which she fired at Daiga hitting him twice yet Daiga had moved on unhurt to catch his plane. How was that possible? Monica asked herself that question on wakening up from her nightmare. She conquered her fears by anticipating that if she were prosecuted for murdering her husband it would be judged a crime of passion and she might be discharged.

She switched on the light and picked up the book Daiga had given her. Why had he selected this bizarre account of the medium being the message? Was he trying to tell her something? The book to her was an enigmatic paradox wrapped in a riddle. She wondered if was meant to drive her mad. She read the message that people missed structural changes in their affairs that were introduced subtly over a period of time. She knew that was true of their marriage. Some of the effects she had been entirely unaware of at the outset. She had not anticipated the cultural consequences. Maybe Daiga was more intelligent than she had given him credit for. Was he trying to confuse her senses? Really drive her mad. And had he not succeeded? She would admit only that she was mad at him.

At 3 p.m. that afternoon she put jeans and a jean jacket over her black T-shirt and put on her sunshade glasses. Then she picked up an old fez cap that she had neglected to use over the years and put it on. The loaded gun was still in her handbag with the safety catch on when she took the bus for the airport. There she went to the Air France desk and asked which terminal passengers would use if flying to Cameroon that evening.

"Terminal1. Go straight right, then left and you'll find it," the agent told her. She didn't have any difficulty locating the terminal waiting room. When she arrived she found a few passengers were already seated and some still coming in. She screened the few passengers in the sitting room. Had she seen Daiga her madness meant that she probably would have gone straight up to him and put a bullet through his heart at close range. As she waited in a corner seat a chill came over her lessening her anger.

"Should I do it?" she asked herself on detecting sweat under her arms.

Then she thought about the money Daiga had stolen and what he planned to do at home in Cameroon with this woman Mungwi. What would her father do if he found out the money was gone. The question vexed her sorely and she decided she had no option but to kill Daiga for his infidelity, desertion and robbery. Three strikes out! What Daiga had done to her she compared to what she thought black men probably regularly did to black girls in Africa. She was no black girl. Was her face not white as snow?

Monica went into one of the airport toilets to inspect her gun. She touched the trigger lightly with her little finger knowing the safety catch was on, replaced the gun tightly in her right jeans pocket not daring to touch the trigger again. She went out of the toilet and sat on one of the chairs behind the door of the waiting room ready for action. She checked her watch at 5.20 p.m. Daiga would surely soon arrive at the airport desk to check in. In a few minutes he would be rightfully dead.

The loud speaker startled her: "Last passengers for Flight 109 Air France with destination Cameroon should kindly proceed to the waiting room Terminal 1." When passengers started streaming out she stood up still anticipating Daiga's late arrival and thinking it might be difficult to draw her gun because it was tight in her pocket. Soon passengers were coming in for another flight. Daiga was surely going to wander in alone and be an easy target. Five minutes later when she realized the Swiss-bound airbus to Cameroon had taxied to the runway did she surrender herself to the Air France information desk. Where was Daiga? Had he flown the coop earlier as Professor Mann had suspected on the telephone. She spoke up boldly at the desk: "I came to meet someone here and to see him off, but I haven't seen him. I wish to know if you can assist me by checking on whether he has left or is still to leave?" This wordy request rather confused the male information agent.

"Which destination are you referring to madam?"

"Cameroon."

"The plane to Cameroon has just taken off bound first for Geneva. Unfortunately, I am not allowed to give information about individual passengers on the flight."

"This person in question is my husband, sir," she informed him curtly.

"That only complicates things. You surely should know whether he has left or not. But let me ask my boss if we can help you. What is your husband's name?"

"Daiga Foncham," Monica told the man who wrote it down and went into an office next door. After five minutes he returned and told Monica: "I can confirm that a Mr. Daiga Foncham left here on July 18 for Douala, Cameroon, via Geneva, on flight 155, Air France."

"What?" exclaimed Monica. "He flew to Cameroon two days ago!"

"Is anything the matter, madam? You look alarmed and pale."

Pale because she realized Professor Mann had been right and she wrong.

Chapter 22

D-DAY

In retrospect, what actually had happened before Monica discovered the ransacked drawer at her home at about 7.30 p.m. on July 18 was that Daiga was already taking his connecting departure flight to Cameroon at Geneva. And when Monica was patrolling the airport at Stuttgart searching out Daiga with a gun on July 20, he was enjoying a meal of corn fufu and jamajama with Mungwi after being welcomed home to his father's compound in Bali.

Sometime in the first week of July, before he had defended his thesis, he had gone to the Air France office.

"May I have the flight schedules for Stuttgart-Douala?" he had asked the agent.

"Do you intend to travel, sir?"

"Yes."

"On what date may I reserve your flight?"

"July 20."

The man looked up the schedule for July 20 and shook his head.

"Sorry, the July 20 flight is fully booked. Maybe you can travel on July 22 or travel through Switzerland on July 18."

"You mean July 18 is good for Douala via Switzerland?"

"Yes."

"Then I take it," Daiga confirmed and the agent had booked him for July 18 instead of July 20.

"But you will have to pay for a ticket before confirmation."

"Can I reserve the ticket in my name?"

"No problem. I will issue a ticket but keep it here. You can pick it up on the day of your flight."

There was just one more important thing for Daiga to do. If he could intercept his father-in-law's cheque from Bonn and clear the equivalent of five million francs CFA, the currency of Cameroon, this would sponsor a royal wedding for him back in Cameroon and make what was now his dream of marrying Mungwi come true.

On July 17, Daiga was doing other things Monica could not have suspected. First, he had called the Sud West Bank from the public phone across the street from the bank.

"This is Daiga Foncham," he had introduced himself. "I call on behalf of my wife and myself. I wish to find out if our cheque from Bonn has arrived?"

"One moment," the bank teller at the other end had said. In a minute the phone had clicked again.

"Hello, the cheque arrived on June 30."

"Thank you. I shall be with you tomorrow at midday."

"No problem."

After this confirmation Daiga back home picked up two shirts, two ties and two suits and pushed them in the boot of the Fiat, telling Monica: "I wish to drop some clothes at the dry cleaner. Do you have anything that needs cleaning?"

"No, I did my dry cleaning last weekend," Monica had told him. Satisfied that he had fooled her, he had driven straight to the airport and paid for a locker. On the way he had bought a small suitcase and pushed clothes and suitcase into the locker, locked it, and returned home. The rest of that day passed without incident though each party had their own secret plans for the days ahead. Daiga's plan was to take off to Cameroon with a hefty wallet. Monica's was to challenge Daiga just before his departure and shoot him dead at the airport.

Then came July 18 and for Daiga D-day. He was due to pick up his attestation of a successful defence in gaining his Bachelor of Arts degree. His flight was at 6 p.m. local time, but he had to check in at the airport at 5 p.m. He had planned to leave the house at 3 p.m. so that he would gain time should there be some unforeseen delay at the university.

Monica, not suspecting any smart move from Daiga that day, was preoccupied with what pleasure she would soon have to see Daiga crawl dying on hands and knees. She was sure she could put paid to his best-laid scheme of betrayal.

At 2.30 p.m., Daiga did one really crafty thing. He took the hedge trimming scissors and using the garden ladder climbed up the outside wall out of Monica's sight and slashed the telephone cable serving their house. He sought to isolate his wife as much as possible that day. After coming around the wall and to Monica's surprise lightly kissing her without saying it was a goodbye kiss, he told her: "I have to pick up my attestation paper from the university. I will take the bus. I should be back in an hour."

"I will be going to my hairdresser," she unsuspectingly replied. "After that we can go out for dinner. In the meantime, I will sunbathe a while in the garden."

All the while that week Daiga had not seen it necessary to check his travel documents. When he went to the drawer he thought he alone used he was shocked and bewildered to find it empty. Not even his Cameroonian passport was there. What had happened to his documents? He saw his whole plan crumble like a house of cards at the flick of a child's finger. It had to be Monica's dirty work. He knew for what reason she might take his travel documents. That would be that she was onto him. He admitted to himself that he had occasionally been careless. Or, at the last moment, had he simply forgotten where he had put his documents? With lightning speed he drew open and searched all the drawers in his room. He pulled down the bags in the walls and wardrobe and searched them too. This did not yield the desired results. The other option was to search the room Monica and he had shared before their marriage started falling apart. That would be risky because she was lying in the sun outside and might at any time come into the house.

He quickly closed his bedroom door when he heard Monica come into the house and enter her room to change her clothes.

He was still thinking of a way out of his dire dilemma when he heard Monica start the Fiat in the garage and drive out probably to have her hair done as she had said. Free from her presence he stepped quickly across the sitting room to her bedroom. There were ten drawers in all. He dragged out nine of them, but found nothing. The tenth drawer was locked. Why would Monica lock one of ten drawers except to hide something? Probably the documents Monica did not want him to find. He rushed around the room, looking on top of tables and chairs and upsetting them in haste and desperation searching for the keys to the drawer. The keys were surely hidden safely away in the purse she always carried with her. No use searching for them. He looked at his watch in panic. The time was 3 p.m. He was fast running out of time.

He still had to go to the university campus, the bank and the travel agency before finally the airport for his flight. Seized by anger and fear he crossed to the kitchen and took hold of the oven poker. He knew he had to act before Monica arrived back home or all would be lost. He pushed the sharp end of the poker between the drawer and the hinge and forcefully levered the wooden drawer open. He dragged it out and hey presto there were his two passports and four letters! He picked up the letters and glanced at their contents. The two were from Mungwi. One was a reply to his first letter to her after the break in correspondence. Another one was her recent letter telling him of the publication of their marriage in church and council. On the other pages were copied his tentative wedding invitation and program of activities that he had prepared at university. So Monica had been monitoring his every step. His secret departure was blown sky high. But he realized his winning card was that she had to have the wrong date of departure since he had changed his flight from that on his program. He wondered why she had never revealed what she knew of his flight from Stuttgart. He grimaced and vowed never to see Monica again. He would vamoose as he had heard sudden flight termed on an American television show.

With this in mind he pocketed his passports, twisted the other papers together, flung them in the trashcan, rushed out and only just caught the intended bus for the university campus. Fortunately for him his attestation was ready. The university secretary simply had him sign and take it. He rushed out again and on time caught another bus for the bank just before closing time.

"I wish to cash some money for some important expenses back home," he told the teller.

She dutifully asked him the account number and how much he needed.

"I need everything in the account though we are not closing it. My wife and I have financial transactions to attend to. We have been in arrears in the settlements of our bills and we are taking a vacation in Africa."

"There are 30,000 Deutschmarks! That is a lot of money to withdraw at one time. I will consult my superior."

Daiga's heart beat like a drum but his alarm was beyond betrayal. When the teller returned she told him he would have to talk to the manager before she could proceed. "Through there, take the door on your left and you will be in his office." A trickle of sweat that had rolled down Daiga's ear to his neck he quickly swept aside with his hand. It would be a nasty situation he knew if the manager refused to give him money that he, after all, regarded as partly his own. His whole plan would crumble. What would happen to him with Monica now surely knowing almost everything? What would he tell her about the broken drawer in her room and the disarray in the house if he did not get away fast on his flight to Cameroon that night?

"Yes, sit down Mr. Daiga. Why do you need so much money?"

"Monica and I have incurred financial costs of late and we thought we would clear off all our bills including final payment of the house and pay some in advance to avoid interest payments because we plan a vacation in Africa."

"I see. Just a minute please. Let me first talk to your wife."

At the back of his mind Daiga had suspected that the manager would not dish out such an amount of money without checking with Monica. Monica was surely back home by now. She usually spent scarcely more than half an hour at her hairdresser for she had very short hair. She probably had discovered the broken drawer and ransacked rooms. He thought again that even if he did not get the money he would catch that flight with what he had. Yet that had not been the plan.

He saw the manager tap the telephone receiver twice and dial again. He congratulated himself on having cut the wire at his home.

"Mr. Daiga," the manager frowned, "something seems to be wrong with your telephone line."

"Sorry about that. There may be a technical hitch. On the other hand we owe the telephone company money. That is why I am here speaking for my wife as well as myself. It is embarrassing to admit the company has stopped our calls."

"Are you really sure you and your wife need all this money. I ask this because your wife came here the other day asking me to be very careful with your family account."

Daiga quickly and with the authority of one talking to a minor replied: "I know about that. I put her up to it. I am saying the same thing. My name is Daiga. This name is on the account number along with Monica's. You know us well. She sought to protect the money for our needs. For three years I have been withdrawing money from this account. Just like my wife I am a legal signatory. She would answer no different from what I am saying. We have to pay our bills urgently and pre-pay our vacation tomorrow."

The manager tapped his pen on the table in a semi-confused state of mind. He finally picked up the receiver and dialed this time to Daiga's relief his teller.

"File the cheque, let Mr. Daiga sign, and then pay him what he needs," he instructed, turning back to Daiga and apologizing. "Sorry for any embarrassment I might have caused you, sir. I just wanted to be sure. You know sometimes we do come across ugly situations so we try to take precautions. Please have a happy holiday in, I presume, your home country of Cameroon."

Daiga smiled saying after shaking the bank manager's hand that he understood the security his wife had sought at his request. Leaving the office he sighed with relief and headed for the teller who immediately presented him with a cheque for signature. The cashier counted out 30,000 Deutschmarks and gave him the money. Daiga asked for a large envelope to put the money in and pushed it below his belt. He crossed the street calmly to a public phone booth and phoned for a taxi to come and take him to the Air France office. There he did not waste five minutes picking up his air ticket. Then he ordered another taxi to drop him at the airport. He looked at his watch. It was 4.30 p.m. He paid off the taxi at the airport and retrieved his suitcase and the bag that contained his two new suits. He entered the nearest airport washroom. Using his handkerchief as a face towel, he rubbed his face and chest down and dressed up in one of his swish German suits. He pushed his Cameroonian passport, some money and his air ticket into his wallet. The rest of the money and documents he tucked away in his suitcase. Then he presented himself at the Air France counter check-in.

It was 5.15 p.m. by the time he had finished his airport tasks. His inner thoughts were triumphant. What a resounding success! Monica would think he was still in Stuttgart the next day. He chuckled over thoughts of better days ahead in Cameroon with Mungwi. The airport loudspeaker came alive and to him a voice pleasantly announced: "Passengers for Air France 318 bound for Geneva, Switzerland, with final destination Cameroon, West Africa, are invited to present themselves at gate 225 for embarkation."

Daiga moved into the flight queue still in a mood of self-congratulation on how he had handled things. He smiled thinking that in a few minutes he would be curtailing what had gone on too long. He knew he was no angel in taking the money and probably did not deserve his good luck in escaping Monica. He wondered if he had been too greedy in taking all that was in the account. In 48 hours he saw himself happily eating fufu and jamajama with Mungwi. After 20 minutes his plane was airborne heading first for Geneva. There, an hour later, he boarded a Cameroon Airlines plane for Douala. He arrived at Douala at 7 a.m. local time and because of insecurity in the city at that hour he waited until 9 a.m. to retrieve his luggage and change enough money to take a taxi to the city 10 kilometres from the airport.

The day was July 19 and Mungwi and his family members were not there to receive him. He knew this was because they had not been told of his earlier arrival. They were instead preparing to journey that evening by bus, arrive at daybreak, and make straight for the airport to receive Daiga. Few private homes in Cameroon villages could boast a home phone else Daiga would have telephoned his change of flight. He just had to make sure that he reached home early enough on July 19 to stop them from taking off on an unnecessary journey. A taxi driver dropped him off at his cousin Willy's house at Deido. Willy, a one-time driver with the defunct Nanga Company, was at home jobless. After much reunion jubilation Daiga took a bath. He changed into one of his other suits and invited his cousin to accompany him to the Cameroon Bank. At the bank he presented some of his German money for exchange. He was surprised at what was given him. Because Cameroon currency value had fallen he had a bonus of 10,000 Cameroon francs.

"I want to buy a Mercedes Benz," he told Willy after treating him to food and wine.

"Okay. Then we go to Hotel le Nde. Nearby you can choose from a good variety of cars."

Near the Hotel le Nde was a second-hand vehicle market where Daiga bought a used Mercedes 190 for three million francs. Even though Daiga was a good driver he invited his cousin to drive him home, an invitation his cousin readily accepted for it would be real fun for him to be the one to drive home such an important person in such a prestigious vehicle and be best man at his wedding. After all Daiga had money on him for everything he would ever need and he expected he would be generous.

They first drove to the shops at Akwa and purchased gifts for everyone in Daiga's family. Daiga bought a valise and fitted it with every precious thing he could find for Mungwi among them a diamond engagement ring, other jewellery, shoes, dresses and underwear. He bought gifts for Mungwi's parents. He paid for everything without a care in the world. His cousin was astonished at his spending spree. Willy wished he could one day pass through such a life before dying. Europe had clearly been really good to Daiga. He began to believe Europe had everything you needed to succeed in life.

By midday they set off on the drive to Bali. At a petrol station, Daiga ordered his cousin to fill the tank. Then he gave him 50,000 francs for his own private needs. His cousin's eyes glowed as he saw the green bills. Willy had not touched or seen so much money in his life. They set off for Bali with Willy driving at a safe speed on what was soon a red sandy road with strips of tar macadam. Daiga was a very important person come home and needed to be considered in this way.

They arrived at Daiga's home at 6 p.m. just when Mungwi and family members were putting the finishing touches together for their trip to Bamenda where they intended to take the Dyna bus for Douala and then a taxi to the airport. There was pandemonium when Daiga arrived early. The festivities started in a flash as his expensive gifts were unwrapped. Mungwi was ecstatic. To her Daiga was a hero. That evening he proposed to her on his knees as he had been taught by Monica. When she accepted him he drew the diamond engagement ring from its box and placed it on her finger.

She asked him shyly where he had got so much money to pay for such fine gifts.

"I won a German lottery!" was his crafty reply.

Chapter 23

RETRIBUTION

Back in Stuttgart Monica cursed the fact that she had been defeated hands down by an inferior adversary. Who did Daiga think he was to treat her in this despicable way? What would Daiga be thinking about her now? She thought he might be thinking how cleverly he had dealt with his dull German wife. She blamed herself for being too late to confront him. She regretted not tackling him earlier. How was her life going to continue? What would she tell close friends and family members about Daiga's disappearance? Her father and mother would ask where he was. Everyone would ask. It vexed her more when she thought that their son was a mixed breed faced with life without a father. Had he been white she could have made up some kind of story to tell him when he came of age. But the stain was on him for everyone to see. Mentally disturbed she picked up her gun and inspected it. The gun had not done the job it was intended for. She had not done the job she intended to do. Now it was too late.

She was tempted to put a bullet in her brain closing the latest whole dirty chapter of her life and leaving the rest for

God to decide his or her guilt. She recoiled from such action. It was not her style. There were two things she could do. Try to rebuild her life and her studies when university resumed and forget about Daiga, or, catch up with him in Cameroon and one way or another level the score. She considered the first option dissatisfying and cowardly. She would never live it down. The second near impossible but with real satisfaction if she succeeded in getting the better of him face to face. But how could she ever do it? If the world were a global village, as the Canadian book had termed it, then it would be possible. Attempting to catch up with Daiga once upon a time would have been an affair of international proportion. Cameroon was so far away, so remote in the third world and his home no doubt beyond her reach in the African jungle. Yet from what she learnt from Daiga it was accessible and that book had encouraged her to believe every part of the world was accessible. She concluded that what she needed was the courage and determination to achieve vindication and retribution in Cameroon.

Her desire for vengeance burned within her like an African bush fire. She pledged to plan meticulously her next moves. In her hours of sensible scheming she determined she would most certainly take gun lessons at a downtown armoury. She immediately picked up the phone then realized it was not working. She wondered if Daiga had been responsible for snapping the phone line and thought how crafty he had turned out to be. The phone could be fixed later. First she would make another trip to Bonn to see her father.

"Money again! Last time it was a gun. Now, it is more money just two weeks after I sent you enough money for the next three months. What are you up to my daughter? I tried to phone you last night but I could not get through."

"No, father, there is no problem. I just thought Daiga and I would go for a vacation out of Germany for a few weeks and it wouldn't be wise to empty our family allowance without telling you. We plan to visit his family in Cameroon if we get something from you to cover the trip. With Burner in your hands we are finally free to go to Africa. I might add that we have finally paid off the house."

This was true. Although it was her father's last payment into their bank account that had paid off the mortgage.

"When do you intend to travel? For the moment my accounts are not very good for my premiums haven't matured and I not long ago put money in your account. If you give me another week I could send you a cheque by express to your bank in Stuttgart. How much do you think you will need?"

Just ten thousand was Monica's rough estimate for air tickets, hotel and transport costs. After all, life in the third world was cheap, she had learned.

"We will be leaving on September 15 and returning September 30 or early in October. Can you and mum continue to look after Burner on his return to school?"

"Yes, we can. Would you tell Daiga that I can arrange him an interview for a job with a newspaper here in Bonn. I believe from all accounts he could be successful in journalism. This could bring the family together. You would be able to study here rather than in Stuttgart and Daiga work. I'll phone and mail him details so he can study the possibility provided I can get through."

"Daiga will be delighted," Monica lied for him. "Now I must go for my plane home. Thanks father."

During the following week of waiting she flew again to Bonn to take her passport to the Cameroon Embassy.

"I want a visa, sir," she told the embassy official thinking it lucky her maiden name was on her passport.

"For when and for how long?" he asked her before photographing her.

"Just two weeks at the end of September."

"What is your mission? Is it tourism or business?"

"Tourism. The visa is for a two-week holiday."

"Are you a family, or single?"

"Single."

"Any arrangements for a tourist guide in Cameroon?"

"Not yet."

"Take this," said the man handing her a brochure. "Inside you will find all the approved hotels in Douala and all the tourism companies that will provide guides for you right to your final destination. All contact phone numbers are there. If you phone them in advance and give them your travel schedule they will help you." The consul stamped a visa on her passport and returned it to her.

Monica decided not to visit her parents but to immediately return to Stuttgart. There she tried to remember what Daiga had drafted as a marriage program for himself and his black wench. The only thing she remembered was that the wedding was to take place in late September. But what date in September? She needed to be present for just retribution on his wedding day. The next morning, when emptying the rubbish, she came across two crumpled sheets of paper. In her hands she saw immediately that this was Daiga's wedding program. She calculated that he must have thrown it in the trash when he ransacked the house. It showed September 21 as the wedding date. She plotted during the rest of July how dreadfully she would avenge his desertion. There would be no misfire this time.

July turned into August at too slow a pace for her. Apart from her gun lessons she wondered what she could do to occupy herself. She found it boring alone in a house Daiga and she had occupied together even when things were going wrong. She cooked alone, ate alone and slept alone. She did not even have the phone fixed. She responded to a letter to Daiga from her father by phoning from the booth across the road to say he was studying it. She occasionally wondered if she was going mad. At other times her head was clear and in a tourist guide she found a detailed map of all the provinces of Cameroon with main towns and villages carefully marked out. She spent August constantly studying the map. There were further details of what official languages were spoken and where. Lucky for her, her parents had taken Burner for a holiday by the sea and were out of the picture. By the end of August she had even worked out the best route to Bali from Douala. This time she decided she would not do the job herself. She would hire a local hit man in Cameroon to bring Daigo to his knees in repentance for his treatment of his true and faithful wife. There had to be someone available in Cameroon to suit her purpose.

One last thing she would do before flying to Cameroon would be to mail a registered letter to herself outlining that the reason for her mission was Daiga's betrayal and marking the envelope to say it should be read only if she did not return home safely to West Germany.

She phoned her father to avoid his trying to phone her and told him in a message during his absence on holiday that Daiga and she were about to leave for Cameroon.

Chapter 24

A SHADY DEAL

Arrangements for Daiga's wedding, the Cameroon wedding of the decade it was locally dubbed, were continuing hitch free.

The arrangements included 20 bridesmaids carrying the bridal train. They would all be dressed in pink linen imported from Nigeria. Mungwi's wedding gown would be 15 metres long. There would be three cars in the wedding convoy. Two white horses would escort the bride's car. There would be parties at four different places in Bali. One would be in Daiga's compound, one in the bride's father's compound, one at Ntfoang Church Hall and another entry unrestricted at the Bali community hall. Champagne brandy and red wines would be available at the family compounds and tankards of beer at the community hall. The church hall party would have soft drinks for children. During the evening two artists from Douala, singers Ndedi Eyango and Salle John, would entertain guests at the community hall gate-free all night.

Daiga, meanwhile, courted Mungwi as no woman had ever been so courted before in Cameroon. He kissed her courteously and declared he would love her forever after they married. Mungwi was in seventh heaven seeing him as a reformed character rich, sensuous and loving. She bathed his feet and promised him undying love. His and her parents were overjoyed when he brought a construction company in to improve their homes.

Daiga also wrote to the Cameroon Ministry of Foreign Affairs with copies of his political science documents and in his covering letter pointed out he was fluid in three languages with experience in Europe. Their reply promised him an interview after his marriage. This had some villagers believing he was even destined one day to become prime minister.

While this was going on in Cameroon, Monica took off from the Stuttgart international airport on September 15 changing her flight in Geneva, Switzerland, on the evening of the same day. Her plane arrived at Douala International Airport at 7 a.m. on September 16 on its usual schedule. Monica had booked by telephone with the Hotel Guave at Akwa. The hotel van picked her up at the airport and she took residence in room 35 of the hotel building's second storey. Her luggage comprised only a small valise carrying two jean trousers, undergarments, two T-shirts, some pictures, a few papers and a written declaration with which she intended to confront Daiga in church. She booked in under her own name of Monica Wonker and spent two days getting to know the hotel staff, especially the lower level staff of cleaners, receptionists and bar tenders. She purchased suitable clothes for backcountry tropical travel at a local shop. She had both American dollars and Cameroon francs.

On the evening of the third day, the 19th of September, she cornered one of the bar tenders and explained: "I am an international detective here in Cameroon for a job and need assistance. I require an escort for my mission out of town who is good with a gun. Can you find me one?"

"But that is a job for the police. As a detective why don't you go straight to the police and request an officer to escort you?"

"At this stage of the job doing so might scare off the criminal I have been after for a year. The police will come in only at point of arrest. The gun will be for defense only."

"I don't know any guy who can do such a job," the barman shrugged and left her. When he had left, Monica saw two other men approach and speak to him. The men then came over to her.

"We learn that you need an escort good with a gun. We know one but you will have to pay us before we bring him to you."

"Oh, yes, introduce me if you are sure he is reliable. I will pay you if I hire him."

"Very good," they assured Monica before she took a $10 bank note from her purse and showed it to them as a deposit. "He is certainly most reliable," they agreed smiling.

"Two of these notes are the deposit fee," one of them challenged her.

"One is all I will give you now. I will be back here after the job is done. You will get the second note then."

"Two of them will then make $20," said the other man accepting her condition.

Chapter 25

KAPTCHEP!

Kaptchep, the deadly armed robber from Dschang, was the man chosen for Monica.

For Kaptchep, there was only one life and that life was his own life. It didn't matter to him how many lives he destroyed to support his life of crime. This one life needed money to keep it going. It was said around the beer halls that he would have killed his mother and father to get money. People believed his philosophy was that people had to die for others to live.

Kaptchep usually robbed strangers of just enough to give him and whatever girlfriend he had in tow a good meal of chicken and red wine in one of the city's top parlours. He could even handle police guns efficiently and he was thought to be paying off policemen. He was a wizard with everything on wheels. He had been heard to boast that with only a screwdriver he could open the door of the Cameroon president's limousine, start it without an ignition key and drive it into the bush. He was a jailbird though and few could count how many times Kaptchep had skipped jail. One judge who had jailed him had mysteriously died soon after. Even though he sometimes stayed in a rented home somewhere in the far quarters of Douala he was far from being free to move at will except at home in Dschang surrounded by supporters. This was because he wouldn't cross a city street in daylight without being frightened by a falling leaf. An oncoming police vehicle by day sent him heading fast for the tall grass. But at night he was king of dark alleys where at gunpoint he compelled his victims to surrender their money and valuables. Such was the person presented to Monica as a safe escort. She had no idea who she was about to take on in the hunt for Daiga.

"My name is Monica Wonker. I am an international detective. I have a job in Cameroon to follow someone and bring him to justice," Monica introduced herself to him. Kaptchep did not very much like the words detective and justice but, lucky for her, Monica added that she wanted to keep the police firmly off the job as much as possible. "At times the police do more harm than good to efficient detective work," she explained to his satisfaction.

"My job is to do what?" he asked her as they sipped tea in a dark corner room of the hotel. "He liked the idea of a white woman being his boss."

"You escort me to Bali and find the man I am after. You bring him to me and your job is by then almost done."

"How far do I go with my gun?"

"Just abduct him, scare him into submission and bring him to me. You won't need to use your gun unless things turn really nasty. I suppose you can drive a car."

"I drive perfectly."

"We will need a hired vehicle and you will be my chauffeur. I shall pose as a tourist and you will be driving me to a site in Bali."

"Why are you after his man?"

"He treated me badly and stole my father's money. I will fill you in on details as we drive to Bali. In the meantime, I will pay you two hundred American dollars. That is half before we leave and the rest when we return safely."

"Okay. We have a deal."

"I understand you have two guns for the job. Can I see them?"

"Why do you wish to see my guns?"

"Just to make sure we are together in serious business."

Kaptchep looked left and right over his shoulders, put his hand in his pocket and brought out two short guns and put them on the table. One was a .38 police gun, the other a locally fabricated double shooter. Do you know how to use a .38?"

"Yes, of course. I have experience with revolvers."

"I shall demonstrate this one for you tomorrow because it has certain intricacies that you may not be aware of."

"It will be fired by you and not by me as a last resort only. That is part of the deal."

"I agree."

"What type of vehicle will we need and how much will it cost?"

"I think we should get a very good vehicle since the police here don't always check the best vehicles. A Land Cruiser for three days could cost us about three hundred thousand francs."

Monica counted out 30 bills of ten thousand franc notes and placed them before Kaptchep. Then indicating she trusted him she pulled out a purse full of hundred dollar bills, took out $200 and handed it to him. "Take this half payment for the job with an extra $30 to purchase a suitable uniform for your role as my chauffeur. Prepare to leave tomorrow morning. I hear it is a six-hour drive."

"Yes," said Kaptchep, hardly believing his takings from what he was inclined to think might turn out to be an easy job. He knew Bali well. He told her how he had once been forced to flee through Bali when his gang made an unsuccessful armed robbery in Bamenda and how they had lost one member to gunfire. He had led his gang to refuge in an inn somewhere in Bali and when things quieted down had returned to Douala via Bafourchu. "That is the roughly the route we will take."

Monica was disquieted by his talk of robbery but she could not turn back their arrangements. "We won't be robbing anyone of money," she simply stated. "You must understand that. You tell me that you are known to the police as a robber. What does that then mean to working for me? You must commit to bringing me back to Douala without a scratch after our job is done."

"I will bring you back and the police will know nothing about it. Our passwords will be *fair play.*"

"No, if you need a password it will be simply the word *love* and don't get any ideas from that. What is your real name?"

"No need for you to know."

Back home that night Kaptchep searched among numerous identity cards and driving licenses he had seized from his victims and found a face on a driving license that resembled his planned disguise. He then went to a barber and had a close shave. At the Nkouloulou market he purchased a Hausa long gown and cap that made him look like a Muslim. With black pencil markings on his cheeks and brows he looked even more like a Muslim from the north. Monica would not have recognized him when he arrived at the hotel the next day had he not come directly to her. She almost had a fit ready to walk away when he sat down beside her whispering *love*. His disguise was perfect. Also useful was the fact Kaptchep was fluently bilingual in the two Cameroonian official languages of English and French and also spoke his Bamileke language.

On the morning of September 20, when they were driving slowly over the Bonaberi Bridge in thick traffic, Monica began to brief Kaptchep on details of the abduction operation,

"The person we are going to abduct is by name Daiga Foncham. He is medium height and brown in complexion. He is handsome with black hair. Actually he will be at his wedding tomorrow in a church known as Ntoafoang Church. Is there suitable accommodation for us in Bamenda?"

"Good enough."

"Then we will spend tonight in Bamenda then tomorrow afternoon, just after midday, drive to Bali. We need a hideout close to the church where the wedding is taking place. A secluded inn or just a private room would suit our purpose."

"I know just the place. I know an inn that is secluded yet fairly near the church," answered Kaptchep. He was thinking of the inn where his gang had taken refuge when they were compelled to flee Bamenda through Bali on that ill-fated night of the armed robbery that gave them nothing.

"How near to the church is it?"

"It is ideally placed. We can go there… then what? You must decide not me."

At this point the traffic got tight at the Foret Bar area and their conversation was interrupted when a policeman came up to them and told them to halt so that a blocked car at the other end could join the road from that end.

"Merde, c'est quoi ca?" yelled Kaptchep, annoyed that the policeman was interrupting his learning of Monica's operational plan. "Yes, you can continue," the policeman, by then aware that a white woman was in the vehicle, said after the traffic cleared.

Monica continued: "I stay in this inn and before the wedding service starts you find a way into the church and fool Daiga into following you out of the church, maybe inviting him to come and get something important for the wedding. You must do the job before the ceremony starts. Maybe there will be an opportunity when he is waiting for the bride to arrive at the church."

"Ah, yes. The bride is always purposely late here in Cameroon but we still have to figure out in exact detail how to accomplish the kidnap. While he is waiting inside the church may be our opportunity."

"I have already thought it out. You will summon him to your secluded vehicle by making him believe one of his relatives has been in an accident on his way to the wedding. If you succeed in getting him into your vehicle you will bring him to me. Luckily, your vehicle has tinted glass. People outside will not see what is happening inside if there are any near. When I have him at gunpoint in the inn I will handle things while you go back to the church to deliver a wedding gift to be handed to the priest. Can you handle that?"

"I could bribe a boy to give him a message to come to the car. But if things go wrong, can I put a bullet in him and speed off picking you up on the way? That might be the most efficient operation."

"No, no, no! That will not avenge the hurt he did to me. That will spoil the operation and risk our chances of returning safely to Douala. We will have our guns loaded only to frighten Daiga or defend ourselves should things by chance sour. He will have no gun so there should be no shooting. One more thing I should let you know is that I am not carrying extra money. I have left almost all my money in a safe back in the hotel with a note so you have to protect me and take me back alive or the game will be up for you. If you lose me you lose money and if you try to rub me out you get very little and the German police will be after you at full speed. I know for instance that your real name is Kaptchep. So, Kaptchep, we will go over further tactics for the abduction tonight in our hotel but it seems the trap is set."

"Don't ever use my name again!" an angry Kaptchep demanded of her. "Use only our password *love*. I consider the job well paid and I don't want to mess it up with dishonesty on my part." He again alarmed Monica by relating from his memory an armed operation carried out in Douala where five of his gang were drawn into a shootout with the police for three hours and finally went home empty handed. He pledged that he was committed to protecting her life then retiring from his life of crime with her payoff. He had secretly ascertained that she was rich and found her sexually desirable and she attracted to him. Why else would she have used the word love. He had thought he might kill the man she was after then abduct her and keep her on his plantation at Dschang as an extra reward for his services. He quickly thought better of that idea in fear of the uproar and attention that might come from German police as she had warned and from his own government.

"Any questions?" she asked to be sure he understood her well enough not to make mistakes.

"For now no questions come to mind. But are you sure the marriage will actually take place tomorrow? What assurance is there that the date or time was not changed?" Kaptchep asked.

"Well, it's unlikely, but you could be right. Something similar happened to me once with the man we are after. If we arrive to find that the wedding has already taken place we just have to draw up another plan to get him. If the wedding is postponed it may even be easier. We would have time to plan it even more meticulously in the limelight and for me the result would likely be just as satisfying." Monica had not thought of the possibilities of change so she improvised her answers as best she could as they drove on to Bamenda.

At this point they reached the Bikoko junction stop. A policeman, seeing their vehicle arrive, jumped out of the shade where he had been sitting waiting and put up his hand. Kaptchep opened the window.

"Documents! And yours, madam," the policeman requested.

Kaptchep fitted a 1,000-franc bill in his documents and handed them to the policeman who flipped through them, removed the money without a word, gave them back to Kaptchep and waved them on without further demand.

They arrived at Bamenda and checked into the Skyline hotel where in separate rooms they were to pass the night. Kaptchep was using the name on his stolen driver's license but Monica used only the word love when addressing him. That night they confirmed that they would bribe a child with a reward to take to Daiga a message that there had been a car accident and for him to follow the boy to Keptchep's vehicle. In the morning, after a breakfast of omelette and toast, Kaptchep asked Monica's permission to take a preparatory recce. "You can come with me if you wish."

"You can go alone but remember that we are taking off for Bali at midday. I heard that it is a half-hour drive from here and that the road is not good."

That night Kaptchep found no response when aroused he knocked at Monica's locked door hoping she might open it and he could make love to her. He reconciled his needs by promising to himself that he would if necessary forcibly bed her on the return journey when she was satisfied by the way he had helped her get even with the man who had wronged her.

He left for Bali Park after they had eaten. His mission was to confirm that the wedding was actually taking place that day. At the park, he chose a woman in a veil at random and told her: "I have come from Douala for a wedding in Bali. I wish to know if it is actually taking place today."

"There is to be a big wedding at two o'clock at the Church at Ntafoang. Musicians from Douala are in town. A cow, fowls and goats have been slaughtered for the wedding feast. The groom returned from Germany rich and his woman is happy and being well looked after. You will enjoy the parties even if you are minority Muslim like me." The woman was more concerned in gossiping about the wedding than answering the question, but she had given Kaptchep firm confirmation.

He returned to Monica to confirm that the time of the wedding was as they had expected and at exactly midday they left for Bali, driving slowly on the muddy road that was not well maintained. Their land cruiser was high enough to carry them with ease over large potholes. They were on the last drive of their mission to even the score with Daiga.

"Remember, never give away my real name in public even in front of this man Daiga," Kaptchep warned her. "I am not unknown in Bali. If you identify me it may mean trouble ahead for you as well as me."

Chapter 26

IT'S AN ILL WIND THAT BLOWS NOBODY ANY GOOD

Way up a hill from the Tsimatua River, on the left side of Ntafoang, stands a certain large bungalow on a ridge. It is a five-bedroom strip belonging to Peter Babila, a recently returned journalism student from the University of Nsukka in Nigeria. He had not built the villa or its row of outhouses. He had inherited it from his late father who had died while he was studying and so had to forfeit any chance of a diploma. After three years back home and unable to find a job on a newspaper or radio station he had thought up a devious way of making money from his inheritance to keep body and soul together.

With help from friends and relatives he purchased beds and bedding and fitted them into the chalets. He rented the rooms out to clandestine and temporary couples at a minimal charge of 1,000 francs for a rest period of about an hour. For the night he charged 2,000 francs. The business hardly flourished but it kept him in money while sending to newspapers and government offices job applications that were rarely or never looked at. Even some dignitaries in town, who wanted a fast one with their latest pick, used his inn for their pleasure and might even rent for a few nights the double chalet in the strip that suited their top-of-the-heap lifestyle.

Babila kept the secrets of his minor success to himself to keep his business growing. There was no government registration or inspections. He cared not who brought whom as long as they paid. He knew some of his customers had other men's wives of good standing with them but he kept affairs secret. There were no elaborate facilities, no food, no drinks and only external toilets to the chalets. There were even no tables. All that was for use in each were a bed, a lamp, two single bamboo chairs, a water jug refreshed each day, a bible and glasses. Visitors could bring other things they thought they might need. The bamboo chairs were beside each bed for the men to place their suits on and the women to lay their dresses on.

This was what Kaptchep called an inn and this was to be Monica's hideout. Once Babila had collected his rent money he handed over the key and showed Monica the chalet with an antechamber. Then he left for a roadside walk leaving her to privacy. He marveled at having a white woman presumably for a date with some important man. Monica was dressed as usual in jeans and jacket and wearing thick dark glasses. When she had paid and Babila was taking his usual walk he saw from the hillside a Muslim man drive off. He wondered if a white man would arrive to take his place.

Kaptchep had no difficulty locating Ntafoang Church, a five-minute drive from the chalets. He took note of the many vehicles parked in the church compound and on the roadside. He reversed his land cruiser and parked it behind bushes at the back of the church facing the return direction. He looked at his watch. It was 1.30 p.m. Perfect timing, he thought, pressing the button to utilize tinted screens. He removed his gun and inspected it. He had given the .45 to Monica and kept the other gun for his own use with cartridges ready for firing. Soon he saw a convoy of three vehicles drive into the church premises. One of the vehicles was a Volvo with wedding decorations and on the number plate the inscription *About to Wed.* White horses and their riders escorted it. He scrutinized the person in the vehicle and did not need to be told that this was the person he had come for. The man was dressed in a well-cut white suit. What should he do? There was no use hurrying. He knew that this man would surely enter the church first, inspect a few things inside, and come out again to chat with a few friends before going back in for the time was still only 1:35 p.m. Fifty metres away some children were playing a heated football match on the rough ground totally unconcerned with what was going on near them. This was perfect for his plan. He could use one of the kids as bait to hook the groom. He got out of the vehicle and moved nearer to a boy watching the game. "My name is Nuyu," the boy replied when he questioned him.

"Well, Nuya, I will send you to the church and pay you 100 francs to buy your biscuit with.Is that okay?"

"Thank you, uncle. I shall go. What do you want me to do there?" the child quickly asked fearing the man might instead engage some other child and that he would lose his 100 francs.

"Just wait. I will tell you when it is time to go to the church and speak to the man who is getting married. Do you know the man?"

"Uncle Daiga. He came back from the white man's country with money to marry Mungwi," the child confirmed.

"I see you speak good English. You will go up to the church altar and tell Uncle Daiga that one of his musicians from Douala needs to see him now. They want to return home immediately because one of them had an accident. Then you must lead your Uncle Daiga to my car behind the bushes behind the church to meet me and talk about the accident. Do you understand?"

"Yes. When will you give me the 100 francs?"

"Say it! Let me hear you say what I told you before I give you the money."

The child repeated word for word what Kaptchep had told him. The boy displayed confidence and inspiration good enough to earn him the promised reward. "Remember it is one of the musicians who had the accident."

Satisfied that the child could do the job, Kaptchep groped for a 100-franc coin in his pocket and handed it to him. He looked at his watch. It was almost two o'clock. He saw an old man come round the corner from out of the church towards his car. He approached him and asked him whether the church ceremony had started.

"You haven't heard the bells, have you? They will wait for the bride to appear before they ring the bells. Only then will she enter the church and the choirs sing and the ceremony begin."

"Thank you," said Kaptchep.

He went back to his vehicle and sat inside leaning on the steering wheel. Soon it was almost 2 p.m., but he still had not heard the bells ring. He nevertheless thought it time the boy went on his mission. He signaled the child and told him to go. The child ran to the church compound and ran back to him again too soon to have delivered the message.

"What happened?" Kaptchep reproached him with a scowl.

"I gave my money to my brother to keep. Some bad boys may take it from me. I am going back to the church now."

"Go now!" Kaptchep drummed into him and there will be another hundred francs if you bring back Uncle Daiga. The child, to Kaptchep's surprise and annoyance, took off away from the church.

Luckily nothing happened until 2.10 p.m. when the bells started chiming and there was action around the church. Kaptchep wondered what he should do. He thought the child might have played a fast one on him and considered going to the church himself to find the groom.

What he did not know was that the child had taken a longer route around the church for his own safety from bullies. Soon to his satisfaction from behind the bushes he saw the child actually coming towards him leading who he judged had to be the bridegroom. He jumped into his vehicle and moved his gun to a reachable place under his seat.

Daiga and the child rounded the bushes and approached the vehicle. The child pointed out Kaptchep to Daiga and ran off probably to start feasting on his easily earned wage and not caring what was happening behind him. Daiga approached the vehicle's window. Kaptchep put down the screen on the passenger side.

"Yes, Mr. Daiga. Am I right? Please just enter out of the hot sun and let me tell you what the bad news is for your musical reception."

Daiga did not hesitate to enter. "Who did the boy say is injured?" he asked bluntly before. Entering the vehicle and sitting down. Kaptchep requested he close the door to drown out the sound of the bells so he could hear of the accident.

"Tell me fast, please. This is most alarming. My bride will soon be in church. I need the musicians for the reception tonight."

Daiga closed the door and heard it lock as Kaptchep pushed the automatic knob beside him to his left. Kaptchep then pressed a screen button to cut any view of Daiga from outside. Quickly he raised his gun and pointed it straight at Daiga's neck

"Hi, what is going on," exclaimed Daiga when the gun touched his neck.

"Mr. Daiga, just cooperate if you wish to ever see your bride again. It won't take long to explain. We have a short ride to take. Don't worry. You are the groom. They won't proceed until you are back at the church. Shift right to the door and put your hands up behind your head. Keep your fingers clasped tight. It's a short ride to meet someone you know who has a message for you. If you try to be smart, I won't hesitate to blow out your brains. Remember, I am steering you as well as the vehicle so make no quick moves or you will die with a bullet in your neck."

Daiga knew that obedience was the only way for anyone with any brains when faced with a gun and such a desperate looking Muslim abductor. "Why are you doing this? Where are you taking me? Are you mad?"

Kaptchep started the engine, pushed the gear into position and slowly drove off. When he reached the entrance to the inn he saw no one around when he stopped. He pocketed the gun but kept it pointed at Daiga.

"Let me warn you again," he told Daiga. "If I have to kill you, you will not be the first. I shoot a good couple of guys like you every other month. So if you don't want to be my next victim, don't play any tricks on me."

After this warning he quickly freed the lock on the doors, jumped out of the vehicle, strode round to Daiga's side and stood a careful distance from it telling Daiga to come out slowly. Daiga opened the door and came out still with no idea who was kidnapping him and why. He sensed the gun was pointed at him from the man's loose pocket and knew the man's finger probably was on the trigger.

"Go ahead to that inn door knowing my gun is pointed straight at your stomach. You are going to meet someone important waiting for you."

"You are wasting your time and mine you know," Daiga said. "If it is money you want I have some on me and you can have it all. I was to be married this very moment. My friends will come to find me. I think you have made a big mistake and you will pay for it if you do not free me."

"You will pay for it if you do not walk slowly into this room now!"

Daiga had no idea who would be waiting for him in such a place on such an important day of his life. He remembered when he had visited the chalets some three and a half years previous and thoughts of the occasion flashed before his mind. It was just before he had left for Europe and the girl in question was a fateful Muslim secondary schoolgirl. He had not even promised her anything she could dwell on that would convince her to return to his life and destabilize his wedding day years later. The brief affair took place when he was doing his second year at teachers college. His conquest was a girl sharing the same campus. Though only 16, she had looked mature for her age. As he walked in front of Kaptcheck he could actually visualize her thick dark hair, rounded breasts and heavy hips. He had that day vowed to taste the juices that were hidden inside this blooming Muslim rose. Was he fated to meet her again after all those years? He knew well the inn's purpose and it had accommodated him.

It was on a certain Sunday during the summer holidays that he had met the girl on the street in Bali and invited her for a soda in one of the village's popular cafes. The girl had turned down the invitation and Daiga had noticed that she was proving to be inexperienced rather than uncooperative as she expressed her fear of being seen drinking in an open place with an African man. Daiga had almost dragged her by the hand to where she had taken an orange juice standing up uncomfortably but enjoying her drink. Daiga had said he would accompany her home. On the way he had tricked her into branching off to greet a friend. The girl had followed him hand in hand not knowing that she was being taken to the very inn and possibly the very chalet now facing him. The girl had not complained when she was in Daiga's arms in bed. Even though he had difficulty convincing her to fully give him what he wanted she had finally done so. And she had performed well even though to his recollection she was a Muslim virgin. After he had given her 5,000 francs the girl had thanked him and gone off perfectly satisfied as far as he remembered. He had met her again twice on the campus but without major incident. Could it be her father who was bringing him again to this inn on his wedding day? Could it be revenge at work on his wedding day? No, there had to be something more devious ahead of him. But what could it be?

When innkeeper Babila saw Daiga walk ahead of the other man his impression was that this man had ordered that the white woman be brought for him. It seemed strange almost incredible considering he knew Daiga and had heard he was getting married that day that hour. He waved to them from a distance without their knowing. Without revealing his surprise he left them as usual to continue his roadside promenade thinking of the stories he could write if only he were a journalist on a newspaper. Was Daiga intending to have sex with another woman on his wedding day? Such a happening he found incredible. He knew Mungwi, too, and he heard the church bells ringing. Despite all he decided to ignore what he was seeing because he reckoned it was not his business to do otherwise.

Daiga tried once more for freedom at the door to the room. "Please, my bride is at the altar in the church. You can hear the bells ringing. I will pay you to let me go and allow you to be an honoured guest at my wedding entertainment tonight."

Keptchep was tempted to ask how much but pitilessly after a pause grunted, "Get inside!"

When both had entered, Kaptchep ordered Daiga to stand still or be shot. He knocked on the anteroom door three times, uttered the password *love* and was answered in the same way to Daiga's astonishment.

"Now, Mr. Daiga, go through this door and meet the person seeking you." Daiga opened the door to find himself face to face across the room with a white woman pointing something at him. He was momentarily at a loss to see who she was in the change of light. "Who are you?" he asked in a whimper as his eyesight started to recover and he saw that she had a gun.

"Your darling wife from Stuttgart," said Monica mocking him. "Yes, Daiga, it is difficult believing who you are now seeing right before your eyes in Cameroon. This is none other than Monica Weber Wonker. I just thought I would pay you a visit with a gift on your wedding day to Mungwi."

Daiga stared in disbelief at the woman he had come to hate intensely and desert harshly.

"Call me the white devil to my face if you dare to interpret your thoughts. This devil loved you just the same. It was you who put the devil in me!"

She spoke firmly though gently and Daiga was frightened by the malevolence he detected in her soft voice. "Sit down Daiga. Push the chair right up to the wall. Sit on it and put your hands behind your head. Don't dirty your smart white wedding suit. Mungwi would be terribly disappointed."

Kaptchep, satisfied that Monica was fully in control, left them alone after confirming that Daiga was unarmed and a safe distance from her. He ordered Daiga to keep his hands behind his head and added that he was just outside and that at any sign of stubbornness or dirty trick he would do his job. "You know what that job is, Mr. Daiga."

"Daiga," Monica continued, "you won a good match with me, right? No. Wrong! You used me like a toilet tissue and flung me into the basin. But I recovered and your deceit has caught up with you. You thought that by abandoning me and taking a plane all the way to Cameroon you could get away with your dirty trick. You were wrong again! Don't you know that the world today is a fairly tiny place? The Canadian book you gave me told me that the world is a global village. You thought that after leaving me for Mungwi I would gnash my teeth then get over it. African girls do just that because they have no tradition except obedience and anyway they don't know what else to do. But I am not an African. I am a Jewish white woman who never forgets. Ask the Palestinians. Now you must pay for your crime."

For a moment Daiga thought she meant money. "I *will* pay if we can come to an agreement. Just tell me how much you want. I still have the money."

"You fool. It is not a return of my father's money that I have come here for," Monica went on relentlessly. "I seek more. You forget that I picked you up from the gutters of Stuttgart, enriched you and that my family did everything to prepare a better life for you and for our son in Germany. After riding me like a horse for two of three years and loading me with a child, you rendered him a virtual mixed race bastard and now you seek to have your cake and eat it by marrying another woman. That crime would make you a polygamist as well. Well, I am here to level the score maybe once and for all if you try to prevent me. You will find out that your lamb has turned into a lion here in Africa. The trouble is that I am confused over what to do with you or to you: whether to lodge a bullet in that dirty skull of yours to stop you from doing again what you did or do something more horrible like getting my man outside to cut you up."

Daiga sat still as a rock kneeling forward with brow behind hands feeling heavier every second. The function of his brain had come to a near standstill at the horror confronting him. He could not think what to say or do to placate Monica. Should he apologize, beg, fight or flee? His options appeared to be hopelessly inadequate. He knew she or the man outside the door would shoot if he struggled with either of them. He had to fight back diplomatically as he was training to do as a promising diplomat. But how could he talk a mad wife and her deadly accomplice out of whatever they intended to do?

"Hi, honey, nothing to tell me?" Monica teased him. "Nothing to say you regret doing? I repeat that you should be sorry for giving me that *Media is the Message* book because it alerted me to the fact that that Cameroon was not so far from Germany after all. Welcome to the global village!"

Daiga failed to understand what she was talking about. He toyed with the idea of again begging for forgiveness by saying he would return her money, but he knew the words would not work. He shook his head in anguish and confusion and when that did not impress Monica one bit he saw that he was in a pot of boiling soup with life or death his option. A last ruse popped into his head. If he could simply knock the gun out of Monica's hand and grab it he could use her as a shield to get past her armed escort outside. He had seen it done successfully by movie stars on American television in Germany. The Muslim outside the room might complicate his escape. He guessed this Muslim man might have money to lose if he did not do the job she had hired him to do. Yet if he reached the open street with people around the man might run away. There on the street he would let Monica go and rush to the church safely surrounded by his friends. Or, he might be killed! He also had a car at the church if he could get to it. But could he desert Mungwi as he had deserted Monica? As those disparate solutions flashed through his brain he calculated the distance between himself and the gun and how many seconds it would take him to lunge for it. Meantime, she ranted on:

"You don't even ask about your son. You just shake your head. Are you not interested in Burner?" She continued pushing him to talk, but just saw his face take on a wry smile at mention of the boy. She saw his lips move slightly but heard no words of regret.

"Now for a wedding present from Kaptchep to your bride," she said, forgetting she had promised not to use her hit man's real name.

"Love!" she shouted out pistol in hand rapping on the door. A glowering Kaptchep barged in nearly knocking her over. "You used my name in vain. I told you not to. It means I must kill him."

"First open that bag and give him the large envelope inside. Thank you! Now go back outside and continuing keeping guard. "Open it, Daiga!"

She jerked the gun upwards at him. "My one bullet will be too valuable in that filthy skull of a rat like you. Open the envelope, I say, and read out the contents. This is my retribution for desertion. After you have read it my man will deliver it to the church for the priest to read to your wedding guests. Start reading now!"

Daiga plucked the letter from the envelope wondering what further devious plot she had devised. It was headed:

A presentation by Daiga's wife, Mrs. Monica Weber Daiga, maiden name Wonker, to be read at Daiga's second wedding to another woman

"My first name is Monica. I married Mr. Daiga in Stuttgart, Germany. The Lord blessed us with one boy by name Burner Schneider. I loved him and my father sponsored all our needs for three and a half years not letting Daiga work so that he could concentrate on studies for his political science degree. The arrangement was that when Daiga graduated from university he would pick up a job and support me to complete my own degree course, which I had had to abandon to stay home to take care of our baby. Last June, Daiga graduated and I was thinking that he would start looking for a job. Instead he turned around and stole our family money, the money my father kept in the bank for us *to pay our rent for more than two years, and all our money for three months of food. He took a plane to Cameroon without my knowledge. Attached are a copy of our marriage certificate, signed in Bonn, Germany, a copy of the cheque Daiga signed illegally to empty our bank account, a photograph of me and my husband Daiga fitting the wedding ring on my finger at Stuttgart City Hall, a photo of me and my husband Daiga performing the matrimonial kiss and a photo of our son, Burner, on his second birthday."*

When Daiga had finished reading he swallowed hard then spoke up. "I admit this is true. So, what do you want me to do?"

At that moment he heard the church bell chime again. He interpreted it as an alarm in the search going on. She did too.

"Okay," Monica said. "The bell tells me I must act fast. To avoid a bullet in the head you will write and sign a note to the priest telling him to read this notice in church before your bride and the congregation. Doing so may permit you to return free to the church. If you refuse you get a bullet in the head."

To Daiga, all options were still equally unappealing. To have such a presentation at the church on his wedding day was a fate worse than death. It would mean the end of his relationship with Mungwi and longer than a lifetime of disgrace. The money he had spent on the marriage would be termed stolen money and Bali people would mock scornfully about it for years to come. Bali men were good at composing songs from people's scandalous deeds. Daiga had even sung one or two of that type of folk song himself. He might go to jail in Cameroon or be deported and jailed in West Germany if word of the stolen money spread. Desperation brought a plan of attack into his head so he stalled for time. "How *is* Burner," he asked in a concerned voice.

"He is with my parents on holiday at the seaside. He has done very well at school. I have to say that he resembles you only in looks. Luckily he has forgotten about the man that deserted his mother."

"Already?"

"He has better things to think about."

"I will come back to you Monica," Daiga appealed as a desperate last resort thinking he might find a kink in her armour of steel. "I loved you too. Let us start anew. No one need know of my indiscretions."

"You make it sound as though I only caught you kissing this African woman when the truth is that you were about to marry her. I shall not even think of taking you back even after your disgrace is apparent in your church before guests at your wedding."

Daiga pleaded: "I promise to deliver your statement peacefully to resolve this problem and return with you immediately to Stuttgart with money to continue our marriage. Will you take this sinner back?"

For a moment Monica blinked in face of his emotional appeal.

Then she smirked: "My man outside, not you, will deliver the truth of your betrayal. You will write a note to the priest as I dictate and Kaptchep will take it to him along with my presentation. He will witness the reading in church and come back here to confirm it was read and maybe you will be free to go to your beautiful African bride *if* she is stupid enough to have you and either way that will be a lucky closure for you."

The name Kaptchep, again spoken forgetfully by Monica, this time jogged Daiga's memory. This was no Muslim man. He suddenly realized he was dealing with the notorious Cameroon bandit and African killer who had created hell in Bali years previous as well as with an insane wife furious with jealousy. Had he been educated in classic poetry he might have been wise while in West Germany to have heeded a verse written by William Congreve in 1697 from *The Mourning Bride*:

> *Heaven has no rage like love to hatred turned*
> *Nor hell a fury like a woman scorned*

But he was not classically educated and had burned his bridges so bad that their love was irretrievable. He realized he had married a strong German woman, drastically underrated her determination and finally turned her mind to vengeance. He had never thought it possible the lengths that his wife might go to in seeking outright retaliation for his taking away not only her pride when he left her but also her father's money. It seemed he was going to pay for his crimes with his life. The villain had become the victim and she had no mercy.

Daiga wondered where such abject fury came from. Then he remembered her mother's critical summary of his character when he had first met her and she had ridiculously characterized him as Germaroon not a Cameroon. Acting defeated he softly asked Monica for paper and pen. "I will do whatever you ask to end this tragedy that will ruin me." His words hid his plan to get the gun out of her hand when he was permitted to lower his hands to write the note. He thought that if he could wrestle the gun from her he might turn the tables and even surprise the fellow outside. He could then justifiably shoot both of them in self-defence on grounds they had tried to rob him and he could temporarily hide the evidence of his polygamous crime under the bed sheets. He had forgotten that the gun held only one bullet. His mind was just as off balance as that of Monica. "Where are the pen and paper?" he asked submissively to put her off her guard.

"Pen and paper are in my purse. Take them out." Monica fully believed she had Daiga negotiating for his life.

Daiga was down but not out and his mind working to save himself. He had noted that her purse had a long attached leather strap and buckle and he intuitively measured the distance from himself to the gun. If he were to sharply flip the bag up under the gun as he moved forward, knock it out of her hand, beat her to any attempt to retrieve it and against the odds win the day.

Monica kept a tight grip on her gun as she waited for Daiga to open the clasp of her purse. She relaxed when he said: "Turn off your hound dog outside and I will love you forever." That said and with lighting speed he upwardly whacked the weapon out of her hand with her bag hitting not just the gun but her chin as well and knocking her head back. She had not expected such smart play with such effect. The gun spun in the air, deflected on the wall, crashed down on the hard concrete floor and exploded. The sound of the blast frightened birds around the area and they screeched off. Cats ran helter skelter in search of a hiding place. Dogs barked and chased something invisible. The blast reverberated on the walls of the inn and even as far as the Ntafoang Church walls. Marie Claire Ashuntangtang, a high school student busy earning a much needed 2,000 francs from her parish priest, the young Father Nicholas Njibaw, in a corner room of the inn, got so terribly frightened that she ended her job badly and seriously risked losing her wages should the man of God further inviolate his sacred vocation by not paying her. But that was the least of it!

Inside the anteroom something worse happened. Monica vomited blood then crashed on the floor face down with a bullet in her throat. Daiga did not realize she was dead. He sat down beside her in shock and fear forgetful of Keptchep. That was not what he had intended. He was so confused and frightened that he forgot about both the hit man outside and he delayed any attempt to snatch Monica's gun from the floor.

Fully a minute later following the shock of the explosion Kaptchep crashed into the antechamber like a tank with gun in front. He glowered down on Daiga like an angry beast when he realized what had happened. He thought Monica must have shot Daiga but found Monica lying dead and Daiga alive.

"I didn't do it! I swear I didn't shoot her. Just an accident," Daiga protested with hands raised before the angry hit man. Had he known Kaptchep better he would have known that this was not the type of man who would listen to any such explanation.

"You shot her? You dirty rat!" Kaptchep muttered with a scowl before triggering two shots to Daiga's head that left him lying on top of his dead wife.

Kaptchep was about to quickly escape the scene but he saw an opportunity. If further money from Monica was lost maybe he would find the money in Daiga's pocket that he had spoken about. He turned to lean down, put a hand in Daiga's inner coat pocket and pull out what was inside. There were cards but there were also bank notes by then stained with Daiga's blood. He did not take time to count the money. He ran to the land cruiser stuffing the money in a side pocket under his Muslim garb, jumped in and started the engine. Glancing at his rear mirror he saw Peter Babila waving and shouting to him to stop and people alerted by the gunshots rushing toward his cruiser. From the side window he blasted off two shots above their heads to scare them off.

Kaptchep sped down the Tsimatua hill. He changed from first through second and third to fourth gear within 200 metres. At the corner his speed had risen to 60 kilometres an hour. In his haste he did not see poorly painted traffic signs warning drivers that there was a narrow bridge ahead and that the maximum speed was 30. Before he reached the crossing he had missed it. The vehicle crashed through one of the arms of the bridge breaking open the front car door. The vehicle nose-dived over the bridge flinging him out. Kaptchep smashed head first into a large stone near the bank of the river but not so seriously that he could not later be identified. The tragic story of Monica and Daiga had further consequences. Peter Babila found her wedding presentation in the room of his inn. He sent the story to a newspaper in Douala, where it made front-page news with the sensational headline:

Three slain at planned wedding of the decade

By Peter Babila

A West German wife, seeking revenge for desertion by her Cameroonian husband, turned a posh wedding at Ntafoang Church in Bali, Cameroon, into chaos and murder.

The groom, Foncham Daiga, who had just returned home to Cameroon from West Germany, and his German wife, Monica Wonker, lay dead at my inn near the church, while his Cameroonian bride-to-be, Mungwi Kah Tita, stood at the church altar waiting for him.

Also slain was notorious bandit Kaptchep who, disguised as a Muslim, had apparently driven the German woman from Douala to Bali to seek her revenge on Daiga.

The two were shot dead in a room at Bali while I was walking in the grounds. Kaptchep was killed when his car crashed over the narrow Bali Bridge as he tried to escape the carnage for which it appears he was responsible...

With Peter Babila's livelihood at Bali lost over the calamity at his inn he had returned to journalism to reverse a misfortune that for him turned lucky since his story with photographs were named the scoop of the year in Cameroon. It went out on the news wires to newspapers all over the world with the *Stuttgart Zeitung* prominently carrying it. To Peter's joy it earned him a fulltime job as a reporter in Douala. It was an ill wind that had blown nobody any good.

Epilogue

A week after the tragedy at Bali two graves were dug in Ba Daiga's compound. Concrete gravestones bore inscriptions. The first read, *"Foncham Daiga, born 1955, died 1982,"* and the second, *"Mrs. Monica Daiga, born 1959, died 1982."*

Mourners from within and outside the Bali region attended twin burial ceremonies photographed by Peter Babila for the Douala newspaper. One sad soul conspicuously, but understandably, absent was Mungwi Kah Tita.

The consequences of their deaths did not end immediately but lived on into a reunited Germany long freed from East-West partition and in a Cameroon independent of colonial rule.

Twenty years had passed when a German man came to the village asking for the home of Mungwi Kah Tita. He was taken to Mungwi's house and with difficulty asked after two graves he had read about in the German newspaper he carried. He wore a metal tricolour Cameroon flag in the lapel of his jacket and showed her newspaper photographs of Daiga and Monica in their youth. She suspected just by admiring his good looks that this man was Daiga's son from Stuttgart.

She took him to the nearby graves she rarely visited where he said a few words in a tongue Mungwi did not understand. He laid lilies beside the gravestones and confirmed what she had suspected.

"Well, Mungwi," he addressed her in English. "Strange things happen in this small world of ours. We really must love one another or, as happened here, die. You could have been happily married to my father but fate did not allow it. I believe that you and my mother loved my father too much. No-one won in the end. That is something to think about. My parents lie here together after losing their way in life and finally separating in death. That is the real lesson for this whole crazy world of ours that may be going in the same wrong direction. Wherever I go, wherever I reside, I shall always take this to be my home. I hope one day to be buried beside my parents and you as some optimistic forlorn act of love defying hate.

Mungwi clasped her hands thinking the young man had come to the end of a prayer and she softly whispered amen.

ञ्ज ञ्ज ञ्ज ञ्ज

Who the writers are

Bill **Fairbairn** is staff writer and a director of the independent community newspaper *Riverview Park Review* in Ottawa. His journalism career since 1950 took in fulltime stints in Britain, Africa, France and Canada. His first job after leaving high school at age 15 was on the *Jedburgh Gazette,* in the Scottish Borders, near where he was born. Then came the *Blyth News,* the *Derby Evening Telegraph,* the *Sheffield Telegraph,* the *Sun,* the *Scotsman,* the *Vancouver Province*, the *Williams Lake Tribune,* the *Montreal Star, Radio Canada International* (CBC), the *Montreal Gazette,* the *Ottawa Citizen* (part-time) and *Legion Magazine.* He also taught journalism for two years on the native reserve near Kamloops, British Columbia, and evening class journalism in Ottawa. Bill spent five years in the 1960s in Africa, working consecutively as a journalist for *The Rhodesia Herald,* now located in Harare, Zimbabwe, the *Northern News* in Ndola, Zambia, and the *Daily Nation* in Nairobi, Kenya. This co-authored book is his third.

befair@sympatico.ca

&c&c&c&c

George Atanga was born in Cameroon in the late 1950s when his part of Cameroon was still a protectorate under Britain. He attended elementary, secondary and high missionary schools in English in the 1970s. He was awarded a Bachelor of Arts degree in English language and modern letters from the University of Yaounde in the 1980s. He has traveled extensively in Africa, Europe and America for work and study. He is now a naturalized Canadian living in Ottawa doing business and polishing up his artistic career in literary and musical arts.

෧෧෧෧